T0374442

# Rainbow's End

## Dorothy Fortune

**BALBOA.**
PRESS
A DIVISION OF HAY HOUSE

Balboa Press books may be ordered through
booksellers or by contacting:

Balboa Press
A Division of Hay House
1663 Liberty Drive
Bloomington, IN 47403
www.balboapress.com.au
1 (877) 407-4847

Print information available on the last page.

ISBN: 978-1-5043-1871-6 (sc)
ISBN: 978-1-5043-1872-3 (e)

Balboa Press rev. date: 12/28/2019

# Chapter 1

Standing in front of the lift doors, he held the beautiful redhead's slim body in his arms, thinking she would be every man's dream. He breathed in her essence. Oh, yes, she was all woman. Raising a hand, he gently stroked her jaw. Then something distracted him.

Looking towards the noise, he stared straight into a mirage of an angel with greenest eyes he ever saw and a gentle smile on her serene face. It left him with the feeling he was swimming in calm waters. Then his body jerked with sensation, or should he say his shaft took control of his body and let him know in no uncertain terms it was ready for action, but alas not with his present company.

The mirage of the angel turned away to finish dressing the display of flowers in the giant urn, her gorgeous auburn hair flowing down her back, and he wanted her instantly. His face flushed for the first time in years like a pimply teenager. Why, because he was holding one beautiful woman and being aroused by another?

God, she was beautiful.

Who was she?

Entering the lift, he decided when he finished showing Leslie her new home for the next seven months; he would make the mysterious woman's acquaintance.

Leslie pulled his face back to her after seeing where his attention had strayed. "Okay, lover, what's caught your eye because you never get that hard for me? Oh my, do I have competition?" Then she planted a tongue-in-his-mouth kiss, jerking back, he saw the other woman watching them in the huge mirror in front of her. Then the lift doors closed.

Wiping his mouth with the back of his

hand he backed away from Leslie "What the bloody hell was that kiss for? You are trouble for me with a capital T Leslie. You know I don't like public displays of affection, now behave yourself"

She laughed at his embarrassment. "Payback's a bitch isn't it"

He cleared his throat to alleviate the husky tone as the doors opened, he moved into the magnificent room without its beauty registering with him. He picked up the house phone and ordered room service.

His interior decorator had furnished the penthouse to his off handed request to 'Make it simple.' So splashes of red to soften the black and white marble. Although he requested the master bedroom be in shades of grey that would enhance the red and grey bedspread that belonged to his grandmother.

Meanwhile downstairs Mary blushed as she lowered her head from the sight of the most handsome man she had ever seen tenderly touching the redhead woman.

Now, always the first to admit she hated men, but this tall man was so full of maleness, of strength, of … sexual … what? She couldn't describe it never having come into contact with this strange emotion, so she sighed and turned away only to see him in the extra-large mirror kissing the woman passionately.

Shrugging her dainty shoulders, she continued with her favourite job. Ah, well, obviously she wasn't ready to…?

What? What wasn't she ready to experience?

# Chapter 2

"He's back again, Mary, that Frenchman. He sure has the hots for you, and he keeps asking for you. I know I get wet every time I see him, he's so sexy" The young girl turned her head and watched through the window as the man strode with confidence towards the florist shop.

*Oh my*, thought Sandy, shifting uncomfortably, His brown hair rested on his pristine white shirt collar under a suit that was so obviously hand-made to fit his large figure like a glove. His coffee-brown eyes laughed at the cheeky young girl behind the counter as he entered the shop. One day he would show this young filly how to play the game, the game of sexual intrigue that is.

Sandy's eyes clouded with need as she stepped in front of him. He was filled with a 100 per cent testosterone and then some, wrapped in the most gorgeous male body, and he knew it. But that didn't stop her. She wanted that body wrapped round her in any way he chose, as soon as possible …please she begged in her sexual activated mind.

Unfortunately at this precise moment, she could see he only had eyes for Mary.

Meanwhile, with her back to the door, Mary tried to still the flutter in her body with a smart rejoinder. "Isn't that you all over? You know I don't attend to customers, Sandy. That's why you were hired. You serve him. I'm off to finish the order for the bride's teardrop bouquet and the boutonnières for the wedding party's immediate family. They need them for tomorrow." Sandy always tried to push Mary into serving on the front counter as much as possible, thinking she needed more practice then maybe she wouldn't be so scared of the customers.

Although Mary hesitated for only a fraction, she heard Sandy giggle. So he was a Romeo as well as a nuisance, and Sandy made no secret that she was just the type of girl to accommodate him.

Heaving a sigh of relief at Sandy standing interference between the man and her, Mary heard Sandy say, "Oh, you are naughty."

Then after a husky, sexy laugh, he replied, "You have no idea, mon petit, how naughty. Maybe one day I will show you and take your breath away."

Sandy gave a sigh of bliss as he touched her cheek. She just loved his French accent.

Mary lifted the small bunch of fragrant flowers with shaky hands and quickly headed for the wet room. So she was right; he was a flirt. She admitted to being worried by the attentions of the big Frenchman, although she refused to let him see it. No way would she let another man have power over her, no matter how gorgeous he was.

Her thoughts drifted back to a week ago, the day he parked outside the flower shop. She could see him through the window, but he just sat in his expensive, open-top sports car. It looked like he was on his mobile phone. He lifted his head and laughed, and Mary felt her stomach muscles clench.

Although it wasn't the first time she had seen him.

Finishing his conversation, he sat for a while. For what she had no idea. Then he got out of his flashy car, entered the shop, and demanded she serve him, calling her by her name.

Mrs Pamela Grant, the shop owner, happened to be in the shop that day and told Mary to go into the back room and she would handle this arrogant Frenchman. She put him right about her staff's duties in no uncertain terms. Some staff attended the front counter. Some were hired only for their expertise in floral arranging. That's what Mary was employed for.

Then Mrs Grant sent him on his way. Mary laughed with her friend at how he backed out of the shop with both his hands up in front of him in a defensive gesture a crooked grin on his handsome face his eyes never leaving Mary's face.

"Later sweet girl"

That was when she felt that strange sensation in her lower regions, like a feeling of... excitement?

Being only five feet five didn't stop Mary. She could be feisty and outspoken with the male population if she was pushed hard enough, but Pammy, as Mary called Mrs Grant, had been calm and patient with the stranger. After all, he could be a future customer.

During her association and friendship with Mary, Mrs Grant thought she was succeeding in her effort to teach Mary to be patient with the men she might meet in her life. Sometimes it looked like a lost cause as Mary hated men ... period, and with good reason.

Arthritis in her hands made it impossible for Mrs Grant to work with her beloved flowers. And the extra weight she carried due to diabetes made it impossible for her to move quickly. In desperate need for more qualified help in the shop, she had seen a brilliant apprentice in Mary at an early age. Mary had watched avidly as Mrs Grant made beautiful displays for the front window and lovely arrangements for her customers.

Now at the tender age of eighteen, nearly nineteen as Mary would remind her friend, it was with care, practise, and lots of patience that Mary learned her craft from her friend. She also showed Mary how to carefully plant the new season seedlings in the huge pots around the outside of the house, and in the vegie and herb gardens at the back of the house in Norfolk.

Mary loved mucking about in the dirt. She told Mrs Grant she loved the feel of the earth in her hands, and going to the country at weekends and holidays was relaxing for her.

As soon as they closed the shop on holidays and long weekends, Mary and Mrs Grant headed to the country, and Mary became a different girl, more relaxed, enjoying her lessons from the other gardeners.

Mrs Grant was worried at first about moving the young girl backwards and forwards from London to Norfolk, hoping it wouldn't interfere with her schooling, but Mary took it in stride.

Mary joined the gardening club at schools and to her delight the head gardener asked Mrs Grant to enrol her to study horticulture online after school. It was an eighteen-month, part-time course with backing from the school for pupils who showed high results and Mary qualified for it.

The grant Mary received was a godsend as she didn't want her friend spending her hard-earned money on her. The school also said they would give Mary extra tuition if required, as the program was more advanced than ordinary gardening. Mary was in heaven.

Seeing how happy Mary was with her beloved flowers in the small garden behind the shop in Islington, planting anything, including more vegetables, made Mrs Grant smile.

After a while, Pamela decided she would have Mary trained at the Covent Garden Academy of Flowers when she was old enough. Knowing the horrendous life Mary had lived, she was determined to give the girl some happiness in her young life. And as Mary loved flowers, then that's where she would begin, learning floristry.

———— ❊ ————

Mrs Grant discovered the eight-year-old girl very early one winter morning, dressed in rags, absolutely filthy, and starving, she was huddled and shivering in the doorway of the shop trying to keep warm.

All the love and loneliness after the death of her beloved husband flowed from the older woman at the sight of this child. She knew she had to help however she could, no matter the consequences. In her heart she felt drawn to help the frail, skinny little girl.

When she was told by her specialist she couldn't have children of her own, Mrs Grant was heartbroken. But she vowed not to let that stop her. With expert advice, she would learn to become a carer to Mary.

It took a lot of years, patience, and gentleness, plus the help of the long serving staff in Mrs Grant's country home in Norfolk and the tranquil gardens that Mary loved. In the early years, they helped a young Mary to finally become their friend and learn to trust her benefactor.

Helping Mary through some traumatic times was an eye opener for the older woman, but seeing the scars down the young girl's back and upper arms, brought the elderly woman to her knees.

A distraught Pamela approached child welfare, showing them photos of the scars, and begged them for more information. They informed her they knew about the bad treatment suffered by the child after the local hospital had treated the little girl from complaints by the schools nurse about the sever bruising on her arms and legs. The hospital had reported the foster parents to the appropriate department for mistreatment and they had been in the process of removing her when she disappeared.

After intensive investigations and research they informed her of the truly horrific life the child had been subjected to.

The court could not prosecute the carer who had inflicted the wounds as he had died in a car accident, but they had enough evidence to prosecute his wife.

Mrs Grant let them know that that excuse was unacceptable, and they had let a small child down and suffer at their lack of management. She told them her lawyers would pursue the case of their negligence of the child's welfare in foster care. A child phycologist was against proceeding with the case because Mary would have to give evidence.

The child's file had been marked closed, not to be opened except by a court order. Mrs Grant advised her lawyers to drop the case in consideration to Mary.

Mrs Grant never let Mary know what she had found out about her earlier life.

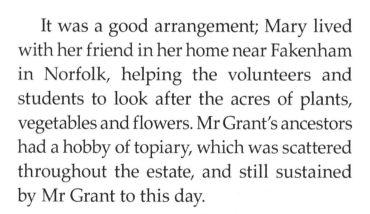

It was a good arrangement; Mary lived with her friend in her home near Fakenham in Norfolk, helping the volunteers and students to look after the acres of plants, vegetables and flowers. Mr Grant's ancestors had a hobby of topiary, which was scattered throughout the estate, and still sustained by Mr Grant to this day.

He also allowed the small local horticultural school to use, and which his wife continued after her husband's death. A few dropped hints by those volunteers that maybe Mary could incorporate learning about market gardening and landscaping as they said she was very good at it.

On winter nights Mary loved listening to her friend reminisce about when her father used to be based at RAF bomber command West Raynham, during the Second World War. He would tell her about driving his British racing green two- seater MG Midget up the tree lined driveway towards the officer's mess.

Even though there was food rationing, they were always fed well, especially if they were going on a night manoeuvres.

The comradely from the other pilots was like a closed club, who had your back, no matter what the circumstances, he remember being brought home many a time inebriated. Mrs Grant actually visited the old airfield; unfortunately it had closed down in the late nineteen ninety's.

# Chapter 3

Mary fell in love with the 18th century Queen Anne mellow red brick twelve bedroom country house, which had been awarded to Mr Grant's ancestors for services and protection to the throne. It sat on a total of one hundred acres of land, surrounded by out-houses, stables, five cottages and array of beautiful bright colourful flowering beds of miscellaneous flowers, shrubs, and citrus trees.

Her bedroom was quite big, decorated with happy pictures on the walls, an old stuffed snuggly armchair that Mary had regularly fallen asleep on. No television as she liked to read books. She loved the feel and the smell of the paper in all her books. Her bed was so comfortable with a flowery light eiderdown for the summer and a heavy Donna in the winter, all in all her peaceful place.

In a happy moment when she was younger she called the place Rainbow Gardens and it is still called that today.

As Mary reached the of age eighteen, she convinced her friend to let her use the small top floor empty flat above the shop as she proved she could manage on her own. Mrs Grant occupied the middle flat so she relented, happy Mary wanted some independence, but she would still be able to watch over her protégée.

Mary tried to make the little flat as homely and cheerful as possible with second-hand furniture and bright cushions and a lovely rug in oriental design from the local charity shops, where she also found two beautiful pictures of rainbows. Again no television but the inevitable books taking up every empty space, on the miniscule fold down table on the squishy old armchair, on her small bed, a very small dining room and kitchen combined.

When she was being paid more money Mary would insist on paying a token rent.

Sighing as she gazed around her little home, at last she had earned her own right to privacy and independence.

There was also the added incentive of the piece of land at the back of the shop that Mrs Grant let Mary use for experiments when she was growing up. Now as an adult she was still learning from her mistakes, like planting bulbs in the right season, and baby seedlings in small containers to take root before putting them in the ground, plus keeping the vegies and salad stuff separate.

It was economical for her and Mary was all for saving money for her own business she hoped to have in the future.

She saved quite a few pounds on growing her own food; it made her proud of her small achievements.

Trying to remember all the advice she had been taught by the experts at home, as she called Rainbow Gardens. Mary didn't have a social life; she saved all her energies for her gardening.

Also she searched magazines and books from the local library to expand her knowledge and listened to radio gurus, plus her gardening club. Mary was relieved she had a lot of help from many sources.

As she grew older she found her ideas changing, trying more 'out of the box presentations' which appear to be successful with the younger gardeners, the older people… not so positive. That would have to be a work in progress.

Being a quick learner she decided she would do a course at the local Technical College after her other studies where finished, improving her knowledge in other aspects of cultivation.

With help from Mrs Grant's patient teaching Mary learned how to drive, and was able to acquire her driver's licence, plus Mrs Grant signed the old van over to Mary, the expense of maintaining the upkeep would be added to the shops expenditure and added to the insurance policy.

This was a good idea as Mary still had to

use it for delivering the floral arrangements and early runs to Covent Garden for fresh blooms. The trust Mrs Grant showed Mary made her feel good, something she never received in any of the foster homes.

Mary had only a few friends, although not in her age group, just Pamela and Doctor Fleming the local female doctor who looked after her health when she was growing up, plus a few older people at Rainbow Gardens, with only acquaintances at the Academy.

---------- ❁ ----------

Coming back to the present, Mary chided herself for wool gathering and set about carrying out her tasks. She loved everything about flowers, the feel, the smell, but most important, the pleasure they gave her.

They wouldn't hurt her, not like some humans, men in particular. No, she refused go back into the dark; sunshine was her 'happy place' now, sunshine and rainbows, always in the light.

Maybe sometime in the future she would be able to relate better to a man, a man that would be gentle and love her and maybe … a big maybe a heartfelt maybe, a future with a child … a happy family her heart cried out for.

Through the years, as a child Mary had the need to know why nobody would love her as she was sent from foster home to foster home. Why she always felt something was missing in her life? She would look in a mirror, expecting to see … what?

Sitting down in her swivel chair, flicking her long auburn hair back into the bun and out of her eyes, she went to roll up the sleeves of her sweater then changed her mind. Even though she was on her own in the room, there was no need to show her ugliness.

Mary laid out the tools needed for the present job on the workbench, then realised she didn't have the wire clippers; searching the two drawers in front of her drew a blank, pushing her chair back and turning away she walked into a wall of solid muscle. "What the hell …" Strong arms went round her waist to steady her.

"At last, I finally have you where you

belong, in my arms as well as my heart my beautiful Mary" Struggling in panic, her heart beating an unusual arrhythmia, Mary screamed in panic… then came back fighting.

Survival instincts she had learned on the streets took over and jumping up in the air, her tiny fists jabbed under his jaw, near his Adam's apple. Staggering back, with tears in his eyes, the man was completely taken by surprise as she pulled his large frame into her body, when she felt him relax momentarily, she then twisted sideways and pushed him hard against the workbench, he let out a grunt of pain.

Mary backed away quick smart, green eyes flashing fire. Hair flying around her head, her little hands shaking but clenched in a fist, up and ready in front of her, but a deep, deep fear lodged inside her.

She knew she was no match for this large and powerful over six foot man, but she would go down fighting.

The man raised his hands, palms forward showing surrender "Desole. S'il vous plait, I mean you no harm, I apologise for scaring you little one, come sit down before you fall down, please be calm"

Unable to stand upright anymore, Mary's shaky legs gave way and she collapsed onto her swivel chair, her body in a cold sweat, lifting her hand to brush her heavy auburn hair away from her sweaty face that had escaped from the bun in her struggle.

Her past came back in a rush, and she immediately lowered her head. Oh yes the foster father had trained her well, with soft words, lit cigarettes and a leather belt.

Her brain had shut down. Her thoughts saying 'Don't look at him, or it would mean another beating' the foster carer's husband had no remorse, and he would punish the little girl at every opportunity, but only when his wife was absent and that was often, not that she cared.

Suddenly shocked back to reality as her dry lips came in contact with a glass pressed to her mouth, swallowing a sip of cold water, she felt slightly better.

Raoul watched in horror at what his thoughtlessness had unfolded, at what he considered a playful caress. He realised the beautiful girl in front of him was terrified, but boy, for a small built woman she put up a good fight, and was ready to knock his block off.

A woman had never refused him, not at any time and it was an experience he did not like. He could make a woman float in ecstasy to the clouds in the sky, just by caressing her.

Yes, he certainly knew how to make a female do his bidding with a soft deliberately placed hand, a soothing word, his sexy smile, of course an expensive gift always went down well and she would be his willingly.

Moreover, he liked his women to have a bit of spunk; they performed so much better in bed. He knew this woman would be a match for him and looked forward to the anticipation already building in his rigid body.

Although at the moment he had some serious apologising to do to this pint size gorgeous woman.

He was mesmerised by her hair flowing all the way down to her waist, longing to touch it. It was the second thing that drew his attention to her, the first being her incredible green eyes. He inhaled her fragrance, what *was* that aroma, why couldn't he place it? His eyes ate her up, and he couldn't get his fill of her.

Leaning forward to breathe in her perfume again, he groaned, rubbing his side, he was sure to have a bruise there when she pushed him into the workbench, but he would allow her to administer to him later, in bed.

He averted his head momentarily to hide his grin, then put a perfectly manicured finger under her chin and felt a kick up his arm as he lifted her head up, and at last his other hand felt the softness of her glorious auburn hair, her green eyes sparkling with tears as she caught his tender gaze.

With an arrogant twist to his lips, he handed her an immaculate white handkerchief as he introduced himself.

"I apologise *Mon infant*, again I repeat I mean you no harm, wipe your eyes, I am Raoul Lafette, drink, its only water" As he tipped up the glass of cold water against her plump lips again, watching as she struggled to swallow the liquid.

He could feel his trousers tent when she licked those juicy lips. After placing the glass on the desk, as he stroked a finger down her silky cheek, he saw her eyes light up. Was it in pleasure … or anger?

Okay, it was anger as she quickly slapped his hand away from her flushed face. Then he saw her beautiful green eyes change to a darker green, mm that's interesting.

Ouch, he got another sizzling feeling from touching her! My God, if he felt that just from touching her, what would it be like if he was actually inside her exquisite body?

Electrifying?

His mind was buzzing with the possibilities, while his body was as taut as a violin string and ready for action.

He definitely wanted this girl naked in his bed, surrounded by his naked pulsing body, a body that had now hardened into an embarrassing bulge in his exquisite fitted trousers.

The sex would be out of this world, the

light and power from their climax would put Piccadilly Circus to shame. He was impatient for that to happen.

He touched her again, her skin texture was so creamy, and he wanted so badly to bend down and lick it, the strawberry red lips were crying out for his lips to kiss them, not realising what he was doing, he leaned forward to do just that, when she pulled away, he looked into her stormy eyes, not showing aggression this time … but fear.

"Get away from me you flaming pervert, don't you dare touch me again or you're a goner, so back off mister" Jerking backwards abruptly, his thoughts confused 'Wow I've got myself a little wild-cat here.' He hadn't unintentionally wanted to cause this woman distress? He had never nor would he ever hurt a female.

Shaking his head while trying to kick-start his brain into gear, and dispel the sensation he had actually caused fear in a woman. It was something that was so distasteful to him.

Moving away from Mary muttering in French, Raoul stuffed his hands in the pockets of his suit jacket; Apology showing in his action, he had to make things right somehow.

He never had a need to force a woman to like him; Women begged for his touch, for his experience in all sexual activities, and he automatically took their attention as his due, after all he was a very much sought after billionaire entrepreneur, and a Lafette, what's not to like.

# Chapter 4

Stepping further back from her, he said "I am already a goner my sweet girl. We appear to have got off on the wrong foot I …" The door slammed back against its hinges, making them both jump.

Mrs Grant barrelled into the room "What the hell is going on here" Looking at Raoul, "Who the hell are you, and what are you doing in my flower room with Mary?"

Seeing the distress on Marys face and her hands clenched in a fist, Mrs Grant rounded on him "Get out before I throw you out, go on, bugger off or I will set the police on you for stalking and trespassing, go on get out" and she pushed and shoved all six feet plus of him. His hands still caught in his jacket pockets, he had no way of holding her off.

Using her enormous weight she continued to push and shove him until he was on the other side of the door which she slammed in his face.

Breathing heavily after her strenuous bout with the stranger, she turned to Mary and hauled her into her arms.

"Are you alright lovey, did that big brute hurt you, if he did, I'll have the police on him like a ton of bricks. Sandy said she heard you cry out?"

———— ❋ ————

On the other side of the door, Raoul shook his head, all desire leaving his body instantly. He smiled at the way he had been manhandled, or should he say woman handled from the room by the big lady using her weight, and boy, did she carry some weight.

Turning to leave he knew he deserved what he got.

Grinning he thought 'No-way would he take on that big mamma'

But still he knew he had been in the wrong, the big woman was protecting her staff member, after all she did not know he would not harm the beautiful girl, he should not have trespassed, somehow he had to make amends

Rubbing his forehead, he thought back at his stupid actions towards Mary, he had seen real fear in her eyes, and felt it in her voluptuous body as she had gone stiff in his arms.

The girl was exquisite in her innocence, and her diminutive figure was a lovely handful. He liked it that she was curvy, her hair a cascade of rippling autumn gold and russet down her spine, although it was her glorious ever changing green eyes that appeared to darken with emotion which caught his attention; they had spoken of defiance, of resilience, then of fear, fear of men, fear of him?

Had he accidently … no, it was not by accident; he had deliberately set out to find Mary on her own in the shop. Approaching the front counter he kissed his fingers then pressed them to the soft lips of the willing Sandy, thanking her for showing him where Mary was.

Smiling he tipped a cheeky wink at Sandy then smacked her on the bottom, "Later sweetness, and I will make your dreams come true" She giggled and said "You're a flirt but I like you, you better not let Mary hear you" And that statement sobered him immediately as he left the shop.

He could not explain why, he only knew he had to find out more about her, why his body came alive just being in her vicinity, and now he wanted to discover what caused so much distress in one so young.

But that would come later; first and foremost he had to get close to her, hmm, how? Thinking hard he knew the more information he acquired about Mary the easier it would be to befriend her. He had just the friend who could help him with that little problem. Looking up the busy road, Raoul decided to walk to the nearest pub and have a glass of wine; he had things to sort out in his head.

Sitting at the bar, he tried to gather his scattered thoughts, trying to understand his actions, but the damn barmaid wouldn't stop bothering him, pushing her very large silicone enhanced breasts forward for him to see.

When he wanted a woman, he was the hunter, not the hunted

Ignoring her was becoming difficult, so quickly finishing a very satisfying glass of his favourite white wine; he walked back towards his parked vehicle, and without opening the door he jumped into his open top fire engine red two seater Italian sports car, thankful the weather was mild for the time of year.

Glancing towards the shop he saw Sandy watching him, and his lazy smile transformed his thoughts to playfulness.

Sandy watched as he waved and blew a finger kiss to the younger girl. Laughing heartily as he saw her pretend to catch it and place it on her lips.

Maybe she would be a good plaything when he finished with Mary. Then he saw Mary and his smile disappeared.

Oooops!

Pausing momentarily before starting the engine, he taped a long finger to his lips; then his mobile phone vibrated in his jacket pocket he viewed the caller and pressed one button.

"Well hello luscious lips, how is my best girl …?"

"Don't you best girl me, you two timing rat, where were you last night, as if I need ask, probably rolling around in bed with a couple of starlets getting your jollies?"

Frowning, how could she possibly know that's exactly what he had been doing? Then he smiled at the enjoyable memory. The twins thought he couldn't tell the difference between them, but they both tasted different.

Shaking his head, okay back to reality, was he supposed to be somewhere special? Damn; now he remembered. They had a fashion show to attend as part of Leslie's undercover job. He was supposed to have been her date to uncover a theft of some special designs.

A designer from one of the fashion

houses he owned suspected espionage and had complained that some of her one-off designs were being copied, so he said he would look into it.

Hence the use of his friend's world renowned detective agency, Ramsey Investigations, and he was given one of their smartest private investigators, the lovely Leslie, who had also become his friend from past involvement.

To say she was a very beautiful woman was belittling her outstanding classic features, Leslie's body was to crave for the forbidden, but and a *big* but, unfortunately not interested in men, women yes, men, a big no, anyway she had become pregnant with the help of IVF treatment to that successful end.

That's why she was at his hotel; he had offered her and her partner sanctuary from the never ending paparazzi that were always on the lookout for juicy news of her famous sculptor partner.

"How can I make enough apologise to you luscious lips, tell me, make me beg, beat me with … no, not that, it makes me want to get down and dirty with you, and you know how I long to get dirty in a hot clinch, but only with you my lovely Leslie"

He screwed up is face at the blatant lies he was telling her, because he knew she was not interested in men which was a shame because she had the most delicious body. A few years back he had tried to seduce her then she dropped her bombshell, *not* interested in men.

She laughed. "Okay playboy, I will get my revenge, and watch you squirm; now how can I help you, no wait are you having trouble with a *woman* and you want my advice?"

"That will be the day I ask you for help, and you know I do not have problems with the fairer sex, actually I do not have trouble with sex either, would you care to try it with me sometime, maybe I could show you some excellent moves... and you phoned me"

She said a dirty word and cut the connection. Laughing at the innuendo she made about where he could stick his sex appendage. Raoul had a moment of uncertainty towards her capability for the work he required now she was pregnant, which was unusual for him as he wore confidence like a shield.

Starting the car, he sat for a moment enjoying the thrill as the engine growled into life, he could feel it throb gently through his seat, then through his body, remembering the first time it happened, he had and still did to this day feel excessive pleasure. Grinning he set off for his home in Knightsbridge.

Raoul Lafette at twenty nine was the younger brother by three years to the esteem French banker Louis, whom he admired immensely. Louis had fought many battles for Raoul until he grew up.

And grow up he did, now over six feet two, broad shoulders and physically fit, with time spent in his home gym at every opportunity, oh yes he had learnt to protect himself.

The boys educated in English private schools, sons of extremely rich parents that had no time for their children. Brought up by staff and various nannies, so when their parent's plane crashed, it was not such an overwhelming loss to the children as they sometimes only saw there parent's maybe twice a year, if that.

He remembered the nannies tried to involve the children with their parents when they were home, but to no avail.

Their father had numerous affairs, which his mother chose to ignore. No love lost between those two people. He remembered his mother saying children cramped her style.

Their mother always travelled with her husband on his business trips, she loved socialising with the other foreign wives, but always let them know she was the wife of the owner, she liked pulling rank on the lower echelons as she called them.

The boys became a self- contained unit; relying only on each other.

In school they competed and excelled in sport and later at university in business and finance. As they grew into young manhood, they also competed for the fair sex, but Raoul did not have the weird appetite for kinky sex his brother still craved to this day.

Raoul drew the females like a magnet, except they never saw the man, only his bulging wallet and how he could help them climb the social ladder, at times this was ok with him as he abhorred the thought of a steady relationship, although he did have a mistress at the moment, she helps him retain the *not available* persona.

His women never complained about the sex they enjoyed, he always made it very, very good for them, making sure they reached their pleasure first before he gave in to his.

Love was a stranger to him, and he would keep it that way, no marriage or children for this confirmed bachelor.

Being sons of generations of bankers, it would not do for them to fail in the profession, even though it was picked out for them by their uncaring parents.

Except in the past year Louis had somehow dropped the reins and was allowing his board of director's way too much say in the running of the bank. Not to say the board members at this time were complaining, they were too busy filling their pockets with questionable deals.

Years ago Raoul had diversified from banking into his own choice career, and moved his business, R.L. Enterprise with great success to Asia and the Middle East, but his headquarters remained in Singapore. One day he would expand to Europe.

Roaring Lion Enterprise, the name of his various businesses, and with diligent financial savvy had made him as rich as his big brother, and he never let him forget it, which made them both smile.

Arriving at his three storied home in Knightsbridge, he parked his car in front of his garage as he was going out again later that evening. Taking the stairs two at a time down to the ground floor, he bypassed the gym and movie and media rooms to the large kitchen.

Opening the small fridge, he poured a glass of his favourite white wine from the family's vineyard. Ignoring the lift he had installed when renovating, he again took the stairs up to the lounge room walking towards the floor to ceiling windows he opened them and moved onto the small terrace.

Shrugging off his jacket he dropped it onto the glass topped table and hooked a straight backed chair with his foot. Straddling it, he sat facing the park across the road. The trees offering shade with their large branches, a few wrought iron garden seats strategically placed, but the piece de resistance was the pond, with ducks to entice the children and visitors to feed them.

Settling into the chair he gave a contented sigh, this house, this home, was his sanctuary.

Sighing with satisfaction at his first sip of the delicious wine, he reviewed the events of the morning. Ok, so things had not gone the way he predicted, time to rethink his actions.

It was obvious to him that Mary had a fear of men.

Why?

How to tackle his next move without causing her stress, with kid gloves obviously. Never having been rebuffed by a female it was a completely new experience for him.

Usually he would buy his woman a

glorious bunch of flowers, take her out for a sumptuous meal, or present her with a whole new wardrobe if he had been with her for any length of time, like two weeks, then take her to bed and show her a glimpse of heaven without involving his heart.

But for some reason not this woman, she called for finesse. So, as she worked with flowers there was no point in sending them to her, so what would a shy woman want from a lover, then his attention was caught by some small children entering the park with an adult, the youngest girl threw her hands in the air and something glittery floated to the ground.

God, how could he be so stupid, of course he knew how to get in her good books, she was a female after all, first and foremost, so he would romance her. He must be more tired than usual, which he was after having travelled in five different countries with different time zones, and then sorting Leslie's problem.

Loping downstairs to his internal garage he parked his car, deciding to sleep on it and start his line of attack with fresh and gentle approaches and a clear head.

Using the stairs again, because he really needed the exercise after sitting for hours on his private jet, he entered his bedroom in a thoughtful mood.

Dropping his clothes on the bathroom floor Raoul leaned against the vanity, his thoughts pensive, and his tongue playing with his top lip as he stared in the mirror.

Was it just a moment of uncertainty that clouded his mind when he had talked to Leslie?

No he was never uncertain; alright he had questions in his head that needed answers. If only he could step back from the problem of Mary Smith. Why was he making this woman important in his life when he could have his choice of any female by pressing a finger on his smart phone?

He had first seen her two weeks ago as she assembled the floral arrangement in the lobby of the Lafette hotel in Mayfair.

He was the sole owner of the hotel but the Lafette Company used it for visiting dignitaries and business VIP's and associates. The penthouse was used by both brothers periodically, Raoul to take his mistress, and other women to and Louis when he visited London for … whatever.

So why did his body come alive, his feelings intensify to a degree of heightened awareness in her vicinity, was it because it was an awakening of something stronger, shaking his head at the doubts manifesting at the situation he found himself in.

He needed to stop doubting himself.

He was Raoul Lafette.

# *Chapter 5*

Casting his mind back Raoul had liked what he saw; the girl with shining green eyes, a tender look on her sweet face. He had no idea who this petite woman decorating his hotel lobby was, but he intended to find out.

Magnificent long auburn hair cascading down her back to her waist, a body that was rounded, no wrong word, it was cuddly. Mon Dieu, what's the blasted word? Why can't I get it right … wait it was shapely, voluptuous, oh yes, it was definitely voluptuous.

It was curved and toned in all the right places, places his restless fingers wanted to explore, and he found it pleased him.

Realizing the front of his pants was stretching he groaned at his lack of self-control. Smiling to himself he looked up expecting to see his curvy angel and realised he was still holding Leslie in his arms, and they were still waiting for the lift.

He hadn't liked it when the young woman glanced at him then looked away as Leslie tongue kissed him, and he knew the young woman saw it.

As this was the first time he had a chance to look over the renovations and refurbishment of his penthouse he wanted to make sure it was of the highest professional specifications expected by the Lafette Company. Then he would leave Leslie to her own devices and introduce himself to the young lady only she had disappeared by the time he returned to the lobby.

Scratching his head in thought, he looked in the manager's office only it was empty. Then seeing the receptionist was not very busy, he questioned her about the floral arrangement. She was full of the information he needed, after he had smiled his 'please help me, little lost boy' smile that got all females in a tizzy.

Later, Raoul would inform the manager to advise his staff to be more discreet about giving strangers information about staff, even if he was the owner but she did not know that.

Back to the beautiful stranger, was it because she looked so different to the woman he usually entertained. They were tall, slim, faces caked with too much make-up which he hated. So many boring women, nothing in their heads, nothing changed with them, they were all clones of each other.

They all knew his rules. No long term relationships, fun dates, fun sex, he always wore protection and never ever relied on the female, he bought them expensive goodbye gifts, no one gets hurt.

BORING, his brain was shouting at him. No more anticipation. No building excitement.

BORING

But with this girl, she had his heart

beating quickly and breathing heavy with just a look, plus it wasn't doing his groin any good, constantly throbbing.

Thinking back to the feeling he got when he touched her in the shop, how it threw his arm backwards with the jolt, his first thought had been 'What the hell'

The awakening that his body spring to life with eagerness, what would he feel if he had her body wrapped round his? No, what would he feel *inside* her magnificent body.

Bliss!!!

Would he feel her wetness acting as a lubricant, coating his penis as her muscles contracting around him the further he pushed himself right into her tight body. The coupling would be electrifying yes, ecstasy, definitely.

He was a Frenchman with a vast experience of women, thanks to one of his older female swimming instructors in high school. At sixteen he was very tall and muscular for his age, and eager to learn, she was a very good teacher, to a very willing pupil.

Yes, he knew how to satisfy a woman,

and he had no qualms in bringing this woman to a mind blowing orgasm.

Blast, considering he was only thinking of her, his arousal was still making itself felt and it was getting more exercise than he was.

Oh yes, he was categorically looking forward to a high octane affair with the delicious Mary, if she had that effect on his body without trying, what would be his response when he had her?

Mind blowing?

If he had not touched her... but he had and he wanted more. All he had to do was get his mind and body under control, at the moment that was easier said than done.

Coming back to the present he looked down at his ragging erection. *Merde* looks like another freezing shower is called for.

Why could he not shake this woman from his head, she was a complete stranger to him, but nothing had prepared Raoul for the strong hold Mary had on his emotions, he could not comprehend this need in him for her, and she didn't even know it.

This woman was a must for him. He must

have her, he must have patience, but first and foremost, he must get her to talk to him and then finally he must convince her to trust him. He had never met a woman who didn't want him, who did not want some part of him, of his body, and he thought cynically, of his overflowing wallet.

Yes, he took his pleasure wherever and whenever it was offered to him, he made no bones about women, he liked them and they satisfied him, but only sexually. He had never met a woman he wanted to keep in his life.

Why had he put up with these other women, when he knew for a long time they were boring him, but he had only realised it when he meet this lovely woman.

This Mary Smith!

Ok, he could go round and round thinking, but it was time for that ice cold shower and with a bit of luck it might cool his ardour. Looking at his reflection in the oversized mirror he observed the bruise on his side, now visible. He'd got that when he hit the workbench in Mary's wet room.

Grumbling, he turned the shower

colder but after five minutes he realized that wasn't working, looking down at his throbbing erection; Raoul grimaced as his hand slowly lowered to his groin.

Rubbing himself dry after a not very satisfying shower, he pondered on a different problem.

His latest mistress, Camille, had been with him longer than any of his other women and although she had known about the women he dallied with in-between her, showed him she was not for him anymore. She had been a good buffer from some of his persistent lovers who wanted more, until they found out about Camille.

Now it was time to break the relationship as he was becoming disgruntled with her sudden possessive attitude, the way she had started dropping hints about moving into his penthouse permanently, leaving some of her belongings scattered everywhere in his other properties he took her to.

So he had his PA take care of disposing of her paraphernalia. Camille had known the rules of their coupling, like the other women he had, fun, sex, and a goodbye gift at the end with no hard feeling, sometimes it worked, sometimes it did not.

That was their problem, not his. He wanted a clear conscious when he pursued the lovely Mary.

He was still friends with a few of his past conquests who were now happily married with children.

Some of their husbands in their younger days had mistresses so there was no problem with the men knowing he had had an affair with their wives when they were single, although the vibes the husbands put out now were hands off.

---- ❁ ----

Going back to the wet room, Mary dropped into the chair in shock at what had happened. Holding her head in shaking hands, she thought just who the hell did he think she was, invading her place of work. Damn the work place, he had violated her *body*. She could still feel his hands as they steadied her before she nearly fell.

Oh he was a very handsome man, a

blush covering her face when she thought of how strong his body felt, a body any woman would love to get her hands on, and probably did seeing the way he trifled with Sandy. She knew he had muscles because she has felt them when she put her hands out to clutch his arms.

All she had to do was remember he was a flirt, a womaniser, a man never to be trusted. If she kept talking to herself, she could be convinced not to take him seriously.

Shame about that!

But she couldn't understand why was he stalking *her*? This was the third time he had come into the shop, so Sandy said, always asking for her, although it was only her second encounter with him.

She wouldn't let the man frighten her simply because she didn't know him, and she certainly wouldn't go down quietly, no man would ever get the better of her again. Mrs Grant bustled in again enquiring "What do you want to do about him lovey, do you want me to inform the police?"

Shocked into awareness Mary had to

think quickly; no way did she want the shop involved in her private disputes.

Mary's anxieties were shown on her face by Mrs Grant statement, jumping up from the chair at the thought of having the police involved frightened her more than the man.

Mary replied in a shaky voice "Oh no please Pammy, please don't involve the authorities, I will sort this out somehow, he must have mistaken me for someone else" Mrs Grant saw how wobbly Mary was, and felt the need to offer advice to her friend, patting her hands as she led her to the office chair.

"Listen girl, you take care, you're too good a friend and a bloody good worker to lose, better than that flighty bit on the front counters, can you imagine her trying to do an exquisite arrangement at one of the society establishments, or at the luxury hotels up the West End.

I have had excellent feed-back on your work from enough sources to value you, even when you were growing up people sang your praises, now off you go, and I will lock up, you can open the shop in the morning please"

A look of surprise on Mary's face said it all, she knew Mrs Grant was happy with her work and a girl could never get enough praise.

Grinning at the kind remark from her employer, Mary closed the front door of the shop then opened the adjoining door and climbed the stairs to her flat.

Sitting later with a cup of Earl Grey, she pondered about the day's shenanigans. She again felt her flesh spasm at the memory of the man's touch. It was a foreign sensation to her. Never had she felt pleasure at a man's touch, pain, yes plenty of times, but pleasure … no never.

He had frightened her when suddenly his arms tightened round her body, she froze, her past never far from her.

Is it because she was a virgin that her body was awakening to feel pleasure from a man instead of pain?

Mary wondered if she would ever be able to have a normal relationship with a man. She did want children, but the mantra continually going through her brain was *how,* if she never let any man get close to her.

How to handle this situation with this particular person was a dilemma. What did he want from her; she was just a simple florist? More importantly, who did he *think* she was?

In the past her body had only ever reacted with revulsion to a man's touch, because she knew she would suffer pain.

So the questions went round and round in her head, why him? Why did she think she could find pleasure from his touch? Would he fill the missing part of her heart, was he what she was looking for when she stretched her hand out to her side waiting … for what, for someone to take it? Was something just out of her reach?

Why did she constantly get the feeling there should be someone beside her?

Could she let him touch her again? She grimaced, then smiled when she realised she was arguing with herself. Hmm she appeared to be doing that a lot since meeting this extraordinary virile man.

Finishing her tea, she emptied the pockets of her trousers for the wash when she came across his hanky. Lifting it to her nose Mary could still smell his cologne, and it reminded her of his abject apologies that she had dismissed in her state of fear. She dropped it into the laundry basket.

Moving into her miniscule bathroom Mary ran a bath, maybe it would help her relax her tense muscles. Sprinkling some of her favourite Rosemary bath oil into the water, she twisted her beautiful auburn hair into a top knot, holding it with a pair of chop-sticks, revealing three broken scars on her back, running from across her left shoulder down to her right hip, plus the burns on both her upper arms from cigarettes.

As she laid her head back, supported with a rolled up face washer she forced her mind to let go of the day's problems.

Only that was impossible, her mind kept going round and round trying to understand why her body seemed to have taken on a life of its own, how it became alert, and how her breasts had tingled when Raoul held her to his big hard muscled body? Her nose wrinkled as though she could still smell his cologne, which of course she could.

The guy was tall, very tall compared to her short stature, crispy dark hair, brown eyes that looked like they wanted to eat her.

His skin sported a nice tan as though he'd been out in the sun too much. His face looked as though he hadn't a care in the world. He could pass as a male model.

Oh and yes he was gorgeous.

Plus he spoke with a captivating accent, racking her brain she thought it sounded like French? Of course it was, hadn't Sandy said 'That Frenchman was here again'

It was a past fear that made her struggle, of being forcibly held down, not by him, her fear was of another perpetrator but she couldn't remember who or why, or separate her fears to this day.

She couldn't work it out? But she would one day. Oh no, that was dark thoughts and she lived in the light now the light was her saviour, so she would look for her rainbow, which always gave her heart peace.

Lost in thoughts she looked at her hands and smiled, they looked like a shrivelled prune, and the bath water was cooling rapidly. Reaching forward she pulled the plug and watched the water swirling away.

At one point when she was younger, she thought that was the way her life was going, down the plughole, until Mrs Grant found her. Mary knew she owed that lovely patient lady a lot for saving her life.

Wrapping her body in a large bath sheet, she rubbed her skin until it tingled. She slipped into her comfy summer pyjamas, giving her hair her usual one hundred strokes, letting her mind drift back to the Frenchman as she prepared for bed. She remembered how civilised and polite he sounded in his apology, his attitude arrogant, plus his manners impeccable.

*Chapter 6*

Opening the shop early the next morning after returning from the flower market, Mary picked up the bundle of letters wrapped in an elastic band off the floor; she would go through it later, after she had unpacked the van if Pamela didn't get the time to do it.

Mary put the final touches to last minute urgent phone and fax orders, before taking her early morning tea-break, smiling at her friend heaving herself onto a stool "Morning lovey, how are you, did you do the post?"

"No, I had a rush order, the mail is on your desk, plus the invoice for these four jobs, would you like a coffee, I am about to make some Earl Grey?" Distracted for a moment, the old lady gave the morning mail a quick glance.

"Thanks, hey hang on, there's a letter addressed to you" her old eyes were full of curiosity as she passed it to Mary.

Her finger shaking as she received the letter, Mary frowned. "I don't know anyone who would be writing to me, there must …"

Ripping the envelope open she is shocked to see silver and gold glitter hearts and stars fall to the floor and a card with hearts all over the front asking for forgiveness, looking inside, the name signed with a big 'R' It could only be from Raoul.

The gift caught Mary off guard, and she smiled.

Showing the card to a puzzled Mrs Grant, Mary asked in surprise. "Do you know anything about this person Pamela?" The elderly woman harrumphed, her lips forming a thin line.

"Oh my, yes indeed, why don't you look him up on the internet, I did? He is a very rich businessman, him and his philandering brother. Born in France and they are known the world over for their cutting edge business acumen, and Raoul for his work in the Middle East. His company is known as R.L. short for Roaring Lion Enterprise.

He is also well known for his exploits with supermodels, actresses, and any other female he can get his hands on, plus his support to various children's charities. You know the old saying, beware of men with a glib mouth, or something like that, are you sure you don't know him?"

"No, I have never met him; you know how busy I have been down at Rainbow Gardens. All I can think of is he has mistaken me for someone else. But if he tries to scare me again he will get a bunch of fives in his handsome face. Now please excuse me and I will make your coffee then I really must get on, I have to deliver the wedding flowers this morning"

Mrs Grant smiled as she walked away; yes Mary was definitely in a fighting mood this morning. She could pity the guy if he walked in now. Then she remembered his size and thought 'The brute's big enough to take care of himself'

Turning the letters over in her hands she didn't see Mary bend down to pick up some of the falling glitter hearts and stuff them back inside the envelope.

It had rained during the morning and as Mary left the shop she glanced up at the sky and smiled as she saw a rainbow fading into the small cluster of clouds.

It turned out to be a very busy day after she returned to the shop because Sandy only worked part-time on Wed, Friday, and Sat morning. Poor Pamela was run off her feet, and had to ask Mary to help on the front counter.

"I know you don't like doing the front lovey ..."

"If you need my help then you have it, just like you have helped me, and let me go to TAFE to learn about plants and landscape and garden design also floriculture, otherwise I would not have had such a great job that I love, come on, let's make some people happy with beautiful flowers"

Smiling at the young couple, Mary

wrapped some baby's breath and half a dozen red roses which she had stripped the thorns off, in bright green and scarlet paper, then handed them to the man who presented them to his girlfriend; the smile she gave him was brilliant as they left the shop their eyes only for each other.

Mary watched wistfully, wondering what it would be like to be loved, and would she ever experience it?

She prayed with all her might that it would happen.

Work got away from her so it was late when she told the shop owner to go and rest after she had finished the bookwork; the poor woman was tired out.

"I might have to hire someone else, since becoming extra busy lately, thanks to your stunning displays; also as I've put on this extra weight I'm really tired all the time, and being a diabetic doesn't help" Pamela muttered as she left the premises. The rest of the day went by so quickly, and it was time to close the shop again. Mary wanted time alone to scrutinise her card.

After finishing off her evening meal of

ham cheese and tomato omelette with a crisp side salad from her garden, Mary sat at her dressing table after her bath, wrapped in a bath towel, slowly given her hair the usual treatment.

She really should get it cut, it was only vanity that made her keep it so long, but she liked her hair long, as it helped hide the scars on her arm and back.

Reaching under her bed for the lovely oriental box she had found in one of the charity shops, she sat on her bed and lifted the lid. Removing the handkerchief belonging to Raoul, Mary lifted it to her face and breathed in his fragrance.

Picking up the exquisite card in front of her, she fingered the glittery stars and hearts and let the events of the other day fill her mind again. In the security of her flat, she knew she had reacted too quickly and angrily to the man's touch, but he had invaded her private space, and his actions that startled her, hmm his actions, but not the man.

Her mind drifted to how tall he was, well over six-feet-something, his hair with a tendency to curl, and very expressive eyes that would talk to a person if they had a tongue, a dimple in his left cheek showing when he smiled, and his skin that had a fragrance all of its own, not unpleasant, just nice.

It was the strength in his body that alarmed her for a minute, for it had been hard to her touch.

Of course his clothes felt very expensive when her hand clutched his jacket, they didn't feel like the cheap material of her clothes.

Recalling his cologne was easy, she still had the aroma in her nostrils, no matter how often she blew her nose, his scent still lingered. Closing the box with her small treasures, Mary slid it back into its hiding place.

She would treasure the things she had of his, or maybe she should give his hanky back to him … or not.

Climbing into her single bed, she again felt a stirring in her female core, clenching her muscles and felt dampness between her thighs. Frowning at this discovery, was she having feelings for this man?

Feelings were a very watered down saying, it was more like a hunger … yes a very good word … hunger.

Shaking her head Mary remembered her colleague saying she could access the computer and maybe she would learn more about the man.

Later, she thought as she snuggled down under the doona, she slipped into a disturbed sleep.

———— ❋ ————

It had been a few years since she had the nightmares; with the help of a very good therapist, she'd learnt how to wake herself up from them before she started screaming.

Unfortunately this was not one of those times, and she woke sweating, her pillow stuffed in her mouth, her throat sore from her screams, the sheets wrapped round her body like she was being tied up.

Breathing deeply, sweat was rolling off her brow as she staggered to the kitchen for some water, her hands shaking as she gripped the glass.

Sitting on the edge of her lumpy sofa, Mary tried to get out of her dark place, but her mind couldn't find the sunshine or rainbows to light the way, she struggled to control her erratic breathing and thought of how the kind lady who had given her a future and saved her life, then she was breathing normally, thinking of her friend always calmed her.

How Mrs Grant had taken the broken child she had been at eight years old and feed her, had cared for her, had given her inner peace and a place to call home.

Her gentleness always made Mary feel wanted, like she meant something to the lady. Mary knew Pamela had become her legal guardian, because she had asked for Mary's agreement, which was whole-heartedly given.

It had been a very important moment in Mary's life when she had said yes, and she would always be grateful to her saviour.

Just thinking of her good luck quelled

Mary's fear and allowed her to return to bed and a restful night.

What she didn't know was Mrs Grant's lawyers had applied for the closed files to be released to Mrs Grant, and then they made a more intensive search than the welfare department had carried out and investigated Mary's life from birth to the present day so she had most the facts on the lovely young girl.

Unfortunately there was a lot of missing files when the cottage hospital burnt down, and her birth information was one of them. Thankfully a midwife had put arm bands on all the babies that night with their names and dates of birth. Pink for the girls named Rose and the other Mary, and blue for the boys, name Joey, Wayne, and David.

Such a sad life for a little girl to be put through, no wonder Mary hated men.

It was courageous of a lady of her advanced years to take on an eight year old homeless street smart girl, but she had, and they had bonded well. Mrs Grant had spent hard earned money to have Mary trained in floristry, and was thankful Mary had grown to respect her mentor.

Mrs Grant had also gifted Mary with her friendship but most of all, her trust and love, and Mary would not abuse that trust, her friend had saved a young girl from the streets, from prostitution and from a life of misery.

Three years ago Mary told her friend some of the deprivation in her younger life and how she ended on the streets. The old lady wanted to hug all the girls hurts away and she never let on to Mary that she knew all the gruesome details from her investigations, but it still shocked the gentle woman at people's cruelty, especially towards children.

Plus Mrs Grant's actions the other day showed a caring mother protecting her young; and she would go to any lengths to protect her friend, which made Mary smile, she had never seen Mrs Grant so feisty.

Mary knew she had to stand up one day and become a whole person, and she was moving in that direction, admittedly very slowly with the help of her steadfast friend, and her therapist, but move forward she would, no more going back.

Pamela Grant had no close family anymore, only a nephew she knew nothing about and had not seen in more than twenty odd years. So she lavished her affection on Mary; knowing at the time that the poor girl had no conception of friendship, of family, of affection, of trust, of love.

So she tried to show her by example through the years that friendship, caring, and trust could be returned if it was given freely, without expecting rewards.

A long while back Mrs Grant came to the conclusion when she had some free time she would change part of her will and bequeath the shop to Mary, as she had already left her the property in Norfolk; after all it was Mary who had put in the time and effort so that the little shop was growing exponentially.

One day Mrs Grant asked Mary to sign some documents at the solicitors, saying it was to protect the shop, but it was actually bequeathing the property in Norfolk to Mary. So if anything happened to her the property in Norfolk was legally Mary's. Yes, she would give her friend a happy and stable future.

Fortunately Mary was trying really hard to overcome her affliction of being shy, hence her brief stints on the front counter. It was strange, but she never felt that way when she was called on to dress a private function, or a church for a wedding, or any of the festive seasons, even at the high-class hotel she had displayed her art. She became lost in her own world of flowers, doing what she enjoyed, making people happy with her floral designs.

It was a very busy few weeks for Mary, but she had heard from the Frenchman via a few lovely friendship cards which brought a smile and she stored them away in her memory box under her bed.

Waddling into shop one late afternoon, Mrs Grant announced they had a large order from the same exclusive hotel in Mayfair, where Mary had been employed once before to do a large floral display in there lobby.

The owners had been very happy with

the display, and one of them had required the shop do a private flower arrangement for a very intimate guest, also it had to be ready for the next evening, which meant Mary would be unavailable in the shop that morning.

Smiling and rubbing her hands, Mrs Grant told Mary this was a huge feather in her cap, as the hotel rarely used outside florists to do there arrangements.

This could bring in more outside contacts for the business, and establish a regular trustworthy presence to the more prominent first class hotels, and that suited Mrs Grant very much. Recognizing expert arrangements her florists were providing were getting positive recognition at last.

Breathing deeply, Mary enquired "Pammy do you think we could be ready in time? The hotel haven't given us much leeway; I would have to be there at least six in the morning to be finished by the early afternoon"

Shrugging her shoulders Mrs Grant sniffed "I will inform the hotel to expect you; it appears the owner is at present in

Paris and won't arrive till late so you won't be disturbed, just try to be out of there A.S.A.P"

Nodding Mary picked up the next order to complete heading for the cold room "I'll put the new supply of flowers from Covent Garden into the fridge, then go on to the hotel by six am"

# Chapter 7

Later that evening Mary was in the small back garden, her mind on the following mornings job as she dead headed some of the late blooms, then picked fresh vegies from her small supply of crops for her evening meal, shivering at the change in the weather, hmm autumn's coming. London had enjoyed a prolonged summer this year, but now the days were getting darker earlier.

Looking at some of the trees in the other gardens, she could see the change of colour in the leaves already; some turning a golden brown, some a darker green, while others were losing their leaves, but the mixture of the colours were beautiful.

Pulling the edges of her cardigan closed she rose wearily to her now cold feet and headed indoors for a warm drink.

———— ❄ ————

Arriving at the hotel next morning, Mary approached the well-groomed receptionist. "Good morning, I have the flowers requested for one of your guests. Can you tell me which room I am to set the display up in please?"

The hoity expression on the woman's face told its own story, looking down her nose at Mary, as though she was not good enough to be in such an exclusive establishment.

Mary was dressed for a morning at the flower markets in blue denim jacket, tight jeans and a shirt that hugged her breasts not realising her outfit enhanced her femininity, raised her eyebrows at the censorious look from the receptionist.

"No one is allowed in the private apartments without the manager's approval. Are you sure you're the florist, do you have some identification please?' Mary knew she had a bit of a cockney accent, but her friend had been teaching her to enunciate properly and her twang had almost gone.

Feed up with the disparaging in the woman's voice, Mary pressed on, handing over her driver's licence "You are expecting an arrangement from 'Pretty Flowers Boutique Shoppe' I have been here before to do an arrangement. I was told to be here before seven in the morning as your guest wants the display set up ASAP, if you can't help me maybe your duty manager can?"

Mary spoke sharply; she could show attitude as well as the stuck-up receptionist.

"Yes, of course, I will get one of the duty manager, please wait here"

She then used the desk phone, speaking quietly to someone. Then she replaced the phone, giving Mary a frosty smile "The duty manager will be here shortly, please take a seat"

It was a while before the assistant manager made a hurried appearance, introducing himself.

"Hi I'm David Holt the assistant manager, you must be Mary Smith from Pretty

Flowers; I'm sorry for the delay, I have just been speaking to the owner of the penthouse, and he wants quote 'A very special display for a very special lady' Unquote.

Smiling he said "Usually our housekeeping would take care of arrangements like special requests from our patrons, but this particular request for your shop to do the presentation came from the hotel owner, and we know your company will do an excellent job, like you did a few weeks ago"

Leading Mary towards the lifts, the manager said "You have to use this lift as its exclusive to this penthouse suite, and you will need this security card to access it. Come and I'll show you up; the guest wishes the floral arrangement to be in place for his special visitor before they arrive later this evening. Please follow me?"

"Mr Holt, did the gentleman give any preference to what flowers he'd like for the lady, is she young or elderly, does she have any allergies to certain blooms?"

The manager shook his head saying "No

sorry, I've no idea, but he said she was very special to him, and please call me David"

"That's no problem, as we at Pretty Flowers Boutique like all our flowers to speak to people. We like the flowers to say welcome and we care for you. At least *my* displays say that, and thanks David"

The look he gave her spoke of tolerance, and he smiled. "Sorry I didn't mean to come across as officious; yes I saw that in the last presentation you did for us, the beautiful cascade of flowers and greenery received a lot of compliments, thank you"

Mary guessed Mr Holt's possibly age was middle thirties, possibly six feet in height, with sandy coloured hair, soft dove grey eyes that shone with humour He had a slight hesitation in his speech, also a barely there limp, but he was friendly. She felt comfortable in his company.

Good, so she was getting better with men, her calming meditations tapes must be working. Grinning at the silly thought, they entered the lift, David using the special key card to access the top floor. The doors slide open so smoothly, with a whisper of sound.

He led her into a foyer area, then to a room at the end of the corridor "Mary, sorry may I call you Mary?" When she nodded he grinned then said "Thank you, now this way to the utility room where there is an assortment of vases all shapes and sizes here for you to choose from for your arrangements, or do I need to supply more?"

Laying the enormous bunches of beautiful fragrant flowers and greenery on the workbench, Mary surveyed the wet room and contents, and then turned to the manager.

"Could I see the main room where the display is to be arranged please?" He thought how confident she sounded, as he showed her the way into the main lounge room.

Mary stopped in amazement; never in her life had she seen such a large nearly empty cold room, and the huge white open marble fireplace didn't add any warmth to welcome a guest. It was a characterless abode.

Nothing to soften the starkness, not even any paintings on the clean flat black and white walls. In what Mary assumed was a sunken lounge were three bright red sofas as the only colour, and what Mary supposed was a coffee table of undistinguishable ugliness separating the sofas.

Wrinkling her nose, she thought 'Yuk, why would a person who lived in a cold sterile apartment like this, bring a special lady friend, and then want it dressed with beautiful flowers? Maybe it was his hidey-hole'

Shaking the disturbing thoughts that were none of her business out of her head, she said "I think this room calls for a display of startling colours, as it gives off negative vibes. As it is for the guest's special lady I know exactly what it needs to bring the room alive. I will put an extra-large arrangement in front of the fireplace to enhance the white marble, so I will need an outsize vase to hold the heavy blooms please"

Just then the manager's phone rang, "Sorry I'm needed downstairs, if you require anything ring through to housekeeping, they would have the larger vases in storage, the number is here on the wall phone" then he was gone.

Scanning the room Mary came to the conclusion she needed more feminine flowers to give the room a lived in look and to break up the sameness of it.

Mary continued to survey the room; then walked to the floor to ceiling windows, seeing the panoramic view of London's beautiful Hyde Park, Marble Arch.

On the left side of the magnificent windows a small hidden bar was located, with a fridge, around the other side of the counter-top, stood three counter high chairs also in black, red and white.

Further along the hallway there were four doors, Mary opened one and stepped inside to what was obviously the master bedroom, and there were two other closed doors, peeping inside one showed a large bathroom, with a bath that could hold a football team, also a very large shower with multiple shower heads. The vanity unit appeared to be made of real marble, but

Mary wouldn't know as she had never seen real marble.

The other one was a walk-in wardrobe that was almost as big as her flat, full of women's clothing, very expensive clothes by the feel of the material.

The dresses were like a rainbow, all different colours, and on the other side of the room, there was shoes to match.

Snatching her fingers away she backed out, closing the heavy door behind her. It was none of her business who the clothes belonged to.

But ... Wow she had only ever seen that amount of clothes in a shop. Looking at the master bedroom, her lips formed a grimace; it was as cold as the main room not welcoming at all.

The only colour in the room was the extra-large bed big enough to have a party in. It occupied the centre of the room and was covered by a bright red and grey Damask counterpane.

Very dramatic and masculine, the walls had light grey velvet wallpaper cover, simply crying out for relief.

The furniture was sparse, consisting of a dark grey upholstered straight back chair, darker grey than the wallpaper. A chaise lounge was situated in front of the large windows, also in the same colour as the chair, and a smarting of small drawers completed the room's décor.

Oh yes, this room was crying out for a woman's touch, and Mary was just the person to brighten it up. Backing out of the room Mary knew exactly what blooms she would use for her display, the lady would be enchanted.

Going into the wet room, Mary set about doing the work she was hired for after receiving the heavy vase from a maid. It was a good job she had brought extra wire for the foliage.

Standing back to survey her work Mary smiled. She had chosen Deep blood red Calla Lilies and seven inch White Heaven lilies to complement each other, and bring the fireplace to life.

The balance was perfect.

It appeared to bring the room alive with the matching of colours. Nodding her head in satisfaction, she then started arranging smaller vases of pale pink and yellow roses in various strategic points around the room.

Yes, a woman would appreciate the colours.

But it was the bedroom that Mary wanted to show the woman she meant something special to the man.

She placed one medium vase of ivory and dark silver leaf foliage with one scarlet rose bud as its centre piece on the bedside table, but her larger display she hung on the wall facing the bed.

It consisted of a larger display of two very large vases sporting branches of Pink Cherry Blossoms

The look was saying to the woman her man thought she was special.

Glancing at her watch Mary realised she had been there for hours so collecting her debris and returning to the reception desk to ask the receptionist for the duty manager, when David appeared out of the office.

"Ah Mary all finished, would you have time for coffee, I would like to ask you more about your work, do you have some extra business cards, so I can acquaint our guests with the company who made the other display they were requiring about. I must say you are extremely professional at what you do. I had a quick look at your work upstairs, and it's beautiful"

Mary smiled at his compliment as they moved to the small table he pointed at.

Smiling Mary said "We already left our business card with you the last time I did an arrangement for the hotel, but I will leave you some more, just in case. It was nice of you to ask, may I have some Earl Grey tea please, I don't drink coffee, thank you"

David waved a hand to a waiter standing behind her chair.

"I have the work invoice for you David, my boss said for you to finish it out after the job's completion and sign off on it please?"

"Yes certainly, have you worked as a florist for long?"

She nodded "Yes, most of my life, my boss sent me to train at the Covent Garden Academy of Florists"

"Have you always worked for the same company?"

Wondering where all these questions were going she answered them tongue in cheek, her personal life was her business, then stood up and extended her hand.

"Thank you for the tea, I need to be on my way"

"Ok, thanks for the cards, now I have to get back to work as well. Mary it was a pleasure meeting you, maybe we could have tea again sometime?"

"I would like that, I have to try and get used to the company of men so my therapist says as I'm very shy with them" He hesitated for a moment then said "Please let me be a friend with benefits, I mean you can feel free to use me as a practice model anytime, Oh Lord that came out wrong?" Smiling Mary thanked him for the refreshments he had provided, but was pleased at his unexpected offer.

# Chapter 8

Smiling again after their talk, and his gaff about a friend with benefits, Mary realised she had been more relaxed in his company, than with any man and happy he was allowing her to practice being sociable with him.

She would benefit from the knowledge on learning how to relax more in male company so yes she would give him a go.

David knew he had no need to see to the invoice himself as anyone of the receptionists could have carried out the simple task, but he wanted to get to know this shy girl.

Mary stowed the rest of the flowers

and greenery that was not required in the van thinking how the manager had made things easier for her with the extra vases.

Oh lord, she found one of the small expensive vases she had accidently picked up mixed with the large leaf greenery.

Mary put her handbag in the front seat of the van, and locked the doors. Turning to go back into the hotel just as a large black limousine drew up.

Giving it a cursory glance as she entered the hotel Mary knocked at the door of Davis's office and at the summons to come in, she smiled tentatively. "Sorry David I accidently picked up one of your vases, should I return it to housekeeping?"

David had just replaced the desk phone. "If you would please Mary, I have just been told by reception the owner and his guest have arrived earlier than expected and are at reception as we speak, sorry got to go"

Mary was delighted to meet the housekeeper, Mrs Lewis for the first time and they chatted for a few minutes. The woman told Mary of the various antics of some of the guests, and of course their off springs as well.

Leaving the office Mary smiled at the compliment she received only to have it fade when she saw who David was talking with ... "Well I never" she silently muttered under her breath.

———— ❀ ————

So the owner of the penthouse suite was none other than Mr Raoul Lafette, who had his arm round the thickening waist of the same long-legged beautiful red-head Mary had seen him with before.

So, if he was in a relationship with this woman and whispering into her beautiful shell like ears, like *he* was, and she was snuggling into his perfect body, like *she* was while he was apparently enjoying it, why Mary wondered, was he trying to get to know her? And why was he sending her lovely cards with glittering hearts and angels.

Her heart plummeted.

Squaring her shoulders as she moved to

pass them she looked him straight in the eyes, his showing surprise while hers was reflecting loathing. 'The miserable sod was two-timing this lovely woman, and I bet she doesn't even know it' Mary thought.

Raoul's smile disappeared in shock when he saw who was walking towards him. As she passed him, he watched the cynicism reflected on her face, and then his brow furrowed deeply in scorn wondering if she knew he would be at the hotel, hell for all he knew she could have followed him.

Then common sense kicked in. Of course she hadn't followed him because he had just returned from Paris.

The woman with him saw how avidly he was watching the young girl as she came close to them, so she kissed him and said "Oh lover, you're so good to me, let's go back to bed again." He dragged his lips from her, frowning and then she moved in really close to him, wrapping her arms round his neck and whispered in his ear "Ah, the same woman of interest to you. Okay, game on lover"

Well of all the cheek, Mary chided

herself, he's just a playboy, romancing any woman he takes a fancy to, well not this woman he ain't.

Mary straightened her back as though readying herself for battle as she walked out of the hotel and sat in her van for a moment to calm her beating heart.

'Cheating bugger' she thought, 'a woman with an ounce of sense wouldn't trust a man like Mr Raoul Lafette, and that includes me, so goodbye to rubbish'

Arriving back at the shop, Mary handed the invoice to the owner, who said she was pleased as she already had received a phone call from the management congratulating her work, saying the customer was extremely happy, and would like Mary to contact him personally.

Hmm, I'll just bet he was Mary thought, while getting the woman he was chasing to decorate his apartment for the woman he was already involved with.

Well screw you Mary thought, her gander well and truly up.

When Mary told her friend what the apartment was like and who the customer was, and who he was with, her forehead creased in worry for Mary, as she knew he was the man who was in her shop and tried to get to know Mary.

"Next time you do an arrangement for that man, I will accompany you, okay, no way are you being left on you own with that philanderer"

Laughing at the old fashioned word Mary replied "No need to concern yourself, remember I told you he has a lovely red-headed slender woman who likes to keep him *very* skin tight close, for all we know she could be his fiancée or even his wife"

Going out to finish unpacking the van, Mary did not want to think about the raw feelings she had when she thought the exquisite woman could be Raoul's other half, so she deliberately kept herself busy with what was left of the day to finish the phone orders.

She would think about her unusual reaction at another time, maybe when her mood wasn't so gloomy.

Why did she let him get to her?

———— ❀ ————

The next day Mrs Grant called out as she came bustling into the wet room. "Mary, have you completed that anniversary bouquet yet, the husband is here to collect it?"

She spied the bouquet on the workbench, already in its presentation gift wrapping.

Sighing Mrs Grant touched the petals. "Oh my Lord, you make the most romantic displays, I know the gentleman will be ever so pleased, come out and meet him"

Mary carried the flowers and presented them to the elderly man. "My dear what a lovely arrangement, my wife will surely see how much I still love her, thanks to your glorious effort. Thank you."

Beaming from ear to ear and her cheeks flushed with his praise, Mary returned to clean up the wet room. After a while Mrs Grant sang out a goodnight.

Just before Mary closed the shop, the phone rang. Damn not another late order. Well she wasn't taking any more orders tonight, they could wait until tomorrow. But when Mary answered it was to hear Raoul Lafette, his strong manly voice stirring her memory.

"Mary, I wanted to phone you in person for the magnificent flowers. You are exceptionally talented as I told the administration here. I would like to take you out to night to thank you in person. I will pick you up at 7.30 ..." Interrupting him Mary said "Your welcome Mr Lafette, I hope you're ... guest approved, also I have no wish to go anywhere with you. You might not have a good reputation to consider, but I do, good night sir" As Mary hung up she heard him curse.

Grinning to herself, Mary slowly walked up the stairs to her little flat, her secure place, feeling very pleased with herself. After her conversation with Raoul, Mary decided to go for walk to the shops and have a pizza for tea, it was very pleasant just sitting in the little café and people watch.

Except her tranquillity didn't last long because she couldn't concentrate as her mind kept returning to the redheaded woman in the wretched man's arms. The first time she had seen the woman, she had been very slim, but the other day she had definitely put on weight. Oh my Lord, maybe she was pregnant?

Okay enough, it was none of her business and it was time to go home and do all the odd jobs one does before bed.

Running a bath full of bubbles, she added her favourite scented oil, Rosemary.

Raising the soft brown Greek Sea Sponge Mary gently washed her very alert nipples. Oh God, all she was doing was thinking about the two timing SOB, and already her breasts were tingling and she felt a sweet sensation down below.

Right she thought, lets sort out why I felt annoyed at the thought that Raoul Lafette may have a fiancée or worse a wife; after all he could have as many females as he wanted, and probably did.

So if he meant nothing to her why was she feeling disappointed seeing him with another woman? If she was honest she had to admit to the attraction she felt for Raoul Lafette, which worried her as she didn't like men … period.

So, again if she was being honest in her *heart*, she knew it was more than attraction, and it scared her a little.

My God, but his hard muscled body had fair rippled with raw sexuality when she touched him.

Whoa, what the hell, she needed to get off this track; she was allowing her thoughts too much freedom where he was concerned.

Mary knew she would never marry, or have children the normal way, unless she adopted, but that was in the future, maybe?

Getting out of the cooling bath she pulled on her pj's, and slid into bed, exhausted; only her thoughts wouldn't give her piece of mind from Raoul Lafette.

Waking the next morning, Mary was still tired as she had tossed and turned most of the night, her dreams of Raoul's soft kisses, which surprised the hell out of her as she had never received his kisses, soft or otherwise.

Wearily she dragged her tired body out of bed at four thirty to get ready to do the early morning run to Covent Garden markets as she promised her employer.

Pulling her long hair up she held it in place with a large clip, no need for a sophisticated style when she was just going to the market, she would fix it properly at work. She might even stop for breakfast if she finished early enough.

Arriving at the packed bustling markets, it didn't take Mary long to suss out her blooms and the vendor threw in some really nice extra-large leaf foliage.

He shared a joke with her about the first time she had gone to the markets with Mrs Grant, when she had enquired when was the best time to get there, he had replied "Well now girly, you would need to be here by Death o'clock" At her puzzled look he tried to explain the old saying in layman's terms.

"Don't worry Missy, it's just an old fable from way back that most deaths happen in the wee small hours, or on the graveyard shift as most shift workers call the 3am hour"

After that Mary always picked the people's brains for helpful hints. Going over to the fruit and vegetable side of the markets for the fresh items she couldn't grow, she stowed her purchases in the back of the van, then walked the six minutes to her favourite place for breakfast, the Counter Vauxhall Arches.

Her purchases would be alright in the van as the weather was cooler now that autumn was nearly over, which had Mary thinking about Christmas, and replanting her little garden.

Half-way through her delicious breakfast, a shadow passed over her table, in the process of drinking the life-saving cup of Earl Grey tea; she looked up into designer sunglasses which she knew obscured dark brown eyes, eyes that had looked at her in the past as if she was his for the taking.

Choking on her sip of tea, Raoul quickly rounded the table to thump her on her back.

Mary with mouth inelegantly open, watering eyes, her voice husky as she exclaimed "Well well, if it isn't the big man himself, just finishing the night, or starting a new day early?"

Then realising she sounded hostile, but unable to retract it, she said "Actually it's none of my business" Reaching into her overly large shoulder bag for a tissue, he interrupted Mary "Yes, your right it is none of your business, but I will allow you this small leeway"

His eyes shadowed when he removed his sunglasses and stuffed them into his jacket pocket.

"Please don't do me any favours Mr Lafette, you must be busy so I won't detain you"

"Did we have something sharp for breakfast this morning, or are we just using me to practice your glib mouth on?"

"Actually I was enjoying breakfast after a busy morning, but now I've gone off it"

"Shame, did you know there are thousands of children worldwide who have never had breakfast, Miss Smith. Who would never see food for a number of days, most of them starving?"

"What are you insinuating"

"That you are wasting food, but that possibly won't worry you, as you obviously have never gone without a meal"

"I have actually gone hungry, so yes I

do know what it feels like. How dare you make assumptions like that when you know nothing about me?"

"Should I apologise. But looking at your gorgeous body I can see you like your food, oh don't get me wrong I like a cuddly woman"

The look she gave him would shrivel up the most robust plant "Yes Mr Lafette, I have seen the woman you like to… ahm cuddly up to. So again please don't let me detain you"

Smiling he reiterated "Why my sweet Mary, I do believe your jealous, how delicious, please show me more of your jealousy as it gives your sad face a gorgeous glow"

# Chapter 9

Mary's mouth dropped opened at this assault on her. Lowering her long lashes so he wouldn't see the shimmer of tears, Mary could vividly remember being sent to bed on many occasions without food, or later scrounging through rubbish bins for any kind of food.

The foster carer's husband took delight in starving the child when his wife was at work.

Oh yes, Mary knew what it was like to go without food, especially when she was on the streets trying to survive at the age of eight.

She looked at this man of substance and

couldn't help her sarcastic remark as she stood up "In your dreams playboy, jealousy is a stranger to me, and looking at you it appears you also enjoy your food so don't be rude, now I have to go"

The smile he gave her was slow and sexy but his eyes still unreadable as he sat her back into her chair, then took the vacant chair opposite, turning it around and straddling it.

"May I, and by the way you are supporting a delicious red bloom to your gorgeous cheeks?"

And then he reached over and ran his finger down her face then sharply released the clip holding her hair, running his finger through it. "I've wanted to touch your glorious hair since I first saw you Mary, it's so beautiful"

At that point she felt heat flood her panties.

Mary's tongue ran away with her before she thought. Jerking away from his hand she quickly rose from her chair again knocking it over in the process; she said "I told you to keep you're wandering hands to yourself mister" Drawing another shaky breath as she backed away from him.

"No"

"No what?"

"No, I won't keep my hands to myself"

"Tough"

"Yes you are"

"What?"

"Tough"

"Will you please go?"

"Again no"

"Why for goodness sake?"

"Because I like talking to you, you are different from the other women …

"Yes as I have said I have seen your *other women*"

"Why, I do believe your still a bit jealous, you lovely little thing you"

"Get real, me jealous over a womaniser like you, I have more respect for myself even if you don't"

Fortunately, or unfortunately as the case may be, Mary's butterflies in her stomach took control and were doing a happy dance with no help from her.

Raoul watched her eyes turn a darker

shade of green, and he could see … what … a flicker of desire in their depth? Raoul knew from their last encounter her eyes changed colour with emotion.

Before Mary lowered her eyes, she saw his smile quickly disappear, his chin lifted in an arrogant gesture, as though she was beneath his contempt, and his eyes held no warmth at all.

Seeing this look, she knew her runaway mouth had scored again.

Yea, score one for the female gender.

For instance, just look at the way he dressed, all haute couture, isn't that the proper word? Oh yes he might try to look casual in his low slung hip hugging jeans and polo shirt with an embroidered horse on it, but she would bet her last pound note they were designer made.

She wondered if he even knew how to buy his clothes, maybe he got his women to order them for him.

He was waaay out of her price bracket. He would be dressed by the best shops in the world, while she dressed in the cheapest clothes from charity shops.

According to the papers and magazines, he had women falling on their knees to be seen on his arm, no doubt about it, but not her.

Didn't she have proof of that herself? No, she definitely should stay clear of him, except he kept popping up on her horizon.

Why? He said he liked her but was that just a ploy to undermine her.

Raoul drew in a deep breath, thinking how predictable she was, how expressive her face showed her emotions all too clearly.

"I have already apologised for my brutish behaviour. I won't apologise again. I would not hurt a hair on your glorious head, apart from my unprecedented need to run my fingers through it" She looked startled at his words as he returned her chair in the upright position by the table, smiling, his eyes no longer cold, his smile took her breath away.

Good, she was unquestionably starting to like him. Obstinate as she was, she would do everything in her power to hide that fact from him, he knew that, but he would chip away at her stubbornness.

"Mr Lafette, I have no experience with men like you …"

"It's Raoul and what do you mean, *men like me?*" Mary met his puzzle gaze, "Well, you're a millionaire, a man of the world, and I don't doubt with huge experience of women so tell me, what do you want with me?"

Mmm pursing his lips, he wondered why she was afraid of men; it had to be something traumatic for her not to see his need for her. He always felt overwhelmed in her presence, his heart beating quickly. His skin had goose-bumps when she was near, like now. He automatically rubbed his arms.

"What do I want with you, oh Mary, I saw you in the foyer of my hotel weeks ago with your beautiful auburn hair flowing down your back like an autumn sunset. I instantly needed to know you, to introduce myself to you, but you had gone by the time I returned. I mean you no harm, ma petite; I just want to know you more. No, that is wrong I want to be a permanent fixture in your life, you have captivated me"

Astounded at what she was listening to, Mary shook her head, "I am just a florist Mr Lafette, and again I ask what would you want with someone like me when you already have a woman?"

He could see the puzzled look in her eyes, puzzled, not fear this time. He would love to tell her explicitly why he wanted her, because her soft rosey red lips were calling for him to kiss, and he desperately wanted to kiss them.

The need for her was growing stronger every day, and it was past time he made his move.

Her womanly scent of rosemary surrounded him when he was near her. He had never seen her wear make-up, not even lip gloss, her face was fresh and clear.

Her nicely rounded figure in jeans hugged the body he wanted, no; *needed* to feel up-close to his hungry body. To remove the cheap tee shirt she had on under her denim jacket, covering her beautiful full breasts, that to must come off so he could fondle them.

He wondered what colour her nipples

would be, a soft rosey pink or creamy like her silky skin. Whatever, he desired his mouth to suckle the protruding nipples … damn and blast; he was so hard he hurt.

Raoul removed his jacket and placed it over his knees to hide his reaction to her. Mary watched him, her eyes drinking in his powerful body.

He moves with such symmetry and in his mannerisms also. Like his hands never fluttered around useless like hers.

Well he just shot that notion out of the water as he started fiddling with the salt shaker between his fingers, like he was playing for time, to distract his thoughts of lust; he lifted his head and looked at her.

"Please Mary, its Raoul; I would like to invite you out to dinner with me one night to show you how sorry I am at my clumsy attempt to meet you. I would also like to put you straight about the woman you saw me with; she is a very important business associate"

Clumsy, him no way did he think she was stupid "Yea, some business associate? You let all your *Business associates* fawn all over you like that with you being an active participant, how charming" Raoul was not deaf to the sarcasm in her voice. "Yes, and I'm Mrs Santa Claus, thank you but no thanks … ah Raoul"

He laughed heartily; at least her comeback didn't have the bite of her other put-downs. She would pay for that quip at a later date, when she was in his bed, quivering and sated after he had taken her to heaven.

Her cheeks flushed at his laugh, startled by the idea that she liked it.

It amazed Mary that he thought she would accept his offer, even if she did feel slightly attracted to him more and more. Under no circumstances would she be a third wheel in his love-life.

Slightly, Mary thought back … Who was she kidding, her butterflies said it was more than slight with their happy dance.

His displeasure at her reply was all over his face. "Do you know your eyes darken to a different shade of green when you're happy, I have never seen that before in anyone? It is quite stunning."

Blushing Mary lowered her eyes, her

hands clutching her serviette in her lap. She didn't want him to see anything in her eyes, especially the attraction she felt for him, or that he was gradually breaching her defences.

"Now may I buy you a fresh coffee ...?"

Mary interrupted saying "Sorry I only drink Earl Grey tea, but no I've had more than sufficient, thanks"

Nodding he continued "As to why I'm here, I had an informal breakfast meeting with one of my friends, I could not believe my eyes when I saw you sitting here, we were meant to meet again, Mon Amie. I will reschedule some of my meetings, and phone you later today about our dinner date" Glancing at his expensive wristwatch he said "Unfortunately I have to leave you now, but I wait in anticipation for our next meeting"

To Mary's astonishment, he did something so surprising it knocked her off balance for a moment.

He lifted her right hand to his lips and kissed her palm, then folded her fingers over it "Keep it safe for me Mon Amie, until I am permitted to open your hand and exchange it for a real kiss of love, with your permission of course" His laughing eyes never leaving her flushed face, "Till later"

Her pulse hammering in her throbbing body, she watched him walk away, his six- feet-plus hard muscled body clad in casual hugging designer jeans that covered his sexy bottom, his polo shirt that fitted his torso like a second skin, the muscles playing across his back as he flipped the leather jacket over his shoulder, holding it with two fingers as he punched the air with his other hand.

He was delicious; she thought as she rubbed her left damp hand down her second hand jeans, her eyes never left his body until he was out of sight.

As he disappeared from her view, Mary lifted the other hand to her mouth and pressed her lips to the spot he kissed her heart beating ten to the dozen. Looking out of the window Mary saw it had started raining, if she looked close she could see her rainbow and it made her happy.

Never in her life had she experience this forceful want, this need her body was going through.

Her nipples tender as they pushed forcibly against her bra, under her charity bought tee shirt, a strange heat had formed between her legs and she found herself drawing the muscles tight in her sex.

Oh my, she thought, oh my. Her expression, if he had looked round would have shown ... stubbornness ... wonder ... but definitely anticipation.

What did he call me, Mon Amie, what the heck does that mean? She wished he wouldn't talk to her in French, but then it was sexy.

So what ... had she agreed to have dinner with him? She couldn't remember as he had scrambled her brain.

Boy was she in trouble; because she realised she *did* want to go out with him. He had started a need in her that was so unfamiliar making her feel important, and special. She was tired of being afraid of her own shadow. She wanted?

Yes she wanted.

Smiling she hugged herself.

Then she recollected the pictures of the women he had plastered to his gorgeous body, in some of her friends magazines and they looked nothing like her.

Businesses associate my foot.

All tall and willowy, long legs, hair and face made up to perfection, jewellery dripping from manicured fingers and wrists and around elongated necks, which she assumed cost the earth, plus all clothed in the latest high fashions that a man like Raoul would demand.

No way did that include her, her shopping for clothes came from Mark and Spencer when she had the spare money, or at the local second- hand shop, not the expensive fashion houses of Europe.

God she was so stupid, how could she have not remembered the gorgeous woman all over him when he was talking to David, the duty manager at the hotel the day she did his flower display?

Okay, when or if he phoned to establish a time for their dinner date, she would refuse his invitation, and remind him he had a girlfriend, and she didn't believe the woman was involved in business with him, unless it was hanky-panky business.

Mary shunned emotional attachments to anyone, the exception being Mrs Grant.

Then a thought occurred to her that she was not as afraid of Mr Raoul Lafette as she normally was with men. What was it about this man that she was beginning to trust, even just a smidgin.

Could he be the man to help her phobia?

*Maybe* he was the man to show her that not all men were bastards, would it hurt her to lower her guard with this man in the future?

Oh boy, that was a biggie.

Ok, she would have dinner with him.

# Chapter 10

A few days later Raoul closed his laptop; he really needed to return to Singapore to take care of business. Also his on again off again mistress Camille, was getting impatient with his absence, hence her constant phone calls, he would not tolerate this harassment, time to end this liaison, he wanted no interference is his pursuit of Mary.

His mind drifted back to the dinner with Mary, when he'd picked her up at the shop, she had on a pair of stone washed jeans, and a soft emerald green shirt, with black sandals. He thought 'The first thing I will do is buy her is a new wardrobe; she definitely did not have the required apparel to go to the places I intend to take her to'

The evening he arrived to take her out to dinner, before she even closed the door to her flat, she was on the attack.

"Are you attached to someone or are you married because I don't go out with men who are in a commitment?" Mary said straight from the shoulder.

He was amazed at the way she came straight to the point, so he owed it to answer her truthfully.

"No Mary I'm not married, and I am not in a relationship with anyone. The woman you saw me with is a very good friend who helps me sometimes in my business as I already explained to you, so please no more doubts."

Mary looked him straight in the eyes "Well you had better not be lying to me. I can't stand liars"

Shaking his head at her forwardness, he helped her into his car, thankful he had decided to end his association with Camille next week. No way was he going to do anything that would jeopardise his having this luscious woman in his life.

Mary sank into the leather seat. "Hmm, I love the smell of leather. This is a beautiful car, ah … Raoul" Blushing furiously as she said his first name, she still faltered at saying it.

He smiled "Yes I am very fortunate to have scored this one as it was designated for another buyer"

"So how did you nick it?"

"Money talks sweet Mary" was his reply.

"Well you certainly have sufficient to make it not only talk, but to yell loud enough to be heard?" she informed him, not without a pinch of sarcasm.

Giving her a crooked grin, he ran his hands round the steering wheel, a dreamy look on his face as he replied "This little beauty was nearly on its way to an Arabian Prince in the UAE, before I saved it"

Shaking her head in disbelief "That can't be right; as that's a desert country isn't it. How can you drive a car on the sand, also this car is not a four wheel drive so it would have been a waste of money?"

Laughing at her interpretation he touched her cheek with a gentle finger "I had to save it from such a desolate future, my sweet, can you imagine this magnificent vehicle covered in sand, ugh, the mind boggles"

He had taken her to one of the many restaurants in Piccadilly, a lovely French one near Shaftsbury Ave.

Mary's happy exclamation at the Art Deco ambience of the place pleased him. "Have you never seen this sort of décor before Mary?" Shaking her head in the negative, she replied "Goodness me, no, I don't go to places like this, it is way out of my budget"

Declining to talk anymore, Mary made her way down the sweeping staircase and into the lower level to the restaurant.

Raoul like the *carte du jour* of this place as you could have casual meals or a 'la carte. He thought a small intimate dinner would be appropriate way to help break the ice and the nervous stance that Mary was displaying.

When he had collected her from the shop

earlier, he had given her a gentle kiss on the cheek. He smiled at the way she blushed.

He meant to ease his way into her emotions and gain her trust. She was such a shy girl but frank in her honesty.

He didn't want to spook her again after he had made the error of telling her he wanted to be in her future, but he would have to be extra diligent not get to close to her, at least not yet, as lately he always had an embarrassing stiffness in his lower region when near her.

The waiter arrived and they discussed the menu.

The meal and evening was a great success, Mary started to lose some of her shyness, until his phone pinged a few times. "Sorry, work." He mouthed at Mary "Hello Les what can I do for you?" Nodding and after a moment replaced the phone in his pocket.

Then he asked Mary about her job and the flowers she worked with. It had the desired effect and she opened her heart describing her job.

"One day, I hope to have my own shop if I

work hard enough, and then maybe go on to do something else like landscaping as I love digging in the dirt, it sooths me. I love all plant life and I try to grow my own veggies. Yes, I like mucking around in the dirt"

Realising she was talking too much about herself, she suddenly clamped up, blushing beautifully. Leaning across the table he gave her a quick kiss on the mouth, saying "I could listen to you talk all day about how you love your flowers"

Mary shyly smiled at his kiss, then she realised she made no move to stop him. Not that she wanted to, and her smile grew wider.

They lingered over an excellent meal, and a bottle of wine, which Mary had no palette for because she had never acquired the taste for wine.

Although this was a nice sweet wine, with a fruity flavour, and yes, after a few glasses she decided she liked it.

Raoul saw her smile "What are you smiling at?"

"Oh I just realised I like my first taste of wine, Raoul why did you kiss me?"

His eyebrows rose at the abrupt question "Because I wanted to drink from your delicious lips, do you mean to tell me you have not tasted this particular wine before? But that is scandalous; it is a very famous drink, known the world over for its delicate bouquet"

"The only bouquet I know about is to do with flowers, Raoul I don't drink wine, I have never had any reason to buy wine, I am saving to buy my own business as I said, I can't afford to fritter my money on incidentals like wine"

"Je ne comprends pas, I do not understand, what is fritter? What does the word mean?" Laughing she replied "It means to waste, to squander"

The look of horror on his face set her off in peals of laughter. "I do not believe this. I would not call the worlds most sought after wine, grown in the most beautiful hills and vineyards in France an incidental. After all it is served in the most excellent crystal goblets in all the exclusive dining rooms in Europe a waste, ah my sweet Mary; I see

I will have to take your education of fine wines into my hands"

As well as other physical things he would definitely enjoy, like her taking parts of his body that is forever aroused around her into her soft warm mouth.

Mon Dieu he was ravenous for her.

Coming back to the present, Raoul smiled as he left his office. Ah yes, a lingering enjoyable activity to look forward to. Feeling uncomfortable, he pulled the front of his bespoke trousers as they tented again at his raging thoughts of this sweet girl.

Yes, the evening had progressed very satisfactory for him, as she had finally relaxed to a degree she allowed him to gently kiss her goodnight, while his unfulfilled body yearned for more.

Using his teeth he deliberately tugged her bottom lip, hearing her give a small moan it took all his strength not to ravish her; his lust for her knew no end.

Except he had been a gentleman and let her go with sweet words "My lovely Mary, dream of me as I will surely hold you in my dreams until our next meeting"

———— ✷ ————

Adding another memento to her little stack of treasures an unused serviette from the restaurant. Sliding her box back under the bed, Mary thought about the evening with Raoul as she lay back against the pillows, he had been very attentive to her, making sure she had enough to eat. Asking if she wanted more wine, informing her where it came from in France. Extolling how it was made, how long it would take to mature, all of which interested her a lot, and set her wondering if she could grow grapes in her garden in Norfolk.

What surprised her most was finding out the wine came from his family's winery.

Then there was the way he automatically assumed she would go to France with him and visit the family vineyards, so she could see the fermentation of the wine personally.

He was a very entertaining dinner host, and she had to admit to having a really good time once she relaxed in his company. They laughed a good deal at the silliest things, and Raoul touched her hand and her face often.

Mary wondered after Raoul had gently kissed her why she enjoyed it so much and were all kisses gentle like his. Raising her hand in a wave goodbye, she watched him drive off in his car with the sudden sensation of missing him.

Oh she knew it wasn't the same feeling she had felt all her life, the feeling that something special was missing from her soul.

This perception was just for Raoul, from her heart. It worried her as she didn't know how to handle what was happening to her.

She would go to the library and do some research, maybe the books would help her.

The next day a box was delivered to her, from a specialty shop in Paris called Mariage Freres; it contained four beautiful canisters of Earl Grey tea.

Oh my … Paris for goodness sake!

There was also a beautiful card thanking her for being an excellent dinner companion, and he would like to have lunch with her today, it was signed simply with a large 'R' Another memento for her memory box.

Also enclosed was his personal business card with a scribbled mobile phone number, with the request to keep the number private.

Working in the back room, Mrs Grant could hear Mary quietly singing to herself. As it was not busy in the front shop, she popped into have a word with her assistant.

"Hello, why are you so happy and how did your evening go with the Frenchman?"

"Sorry, did I disturb you, oh Pammy you would not believe it. I had a most exciting night; the dinner had been great, but I wasn't fussed about the wine at first Raoul said he would teach me how to appric … I can't think of the words he used, except I would like the wines he chose"

Her friend had a worried look on her face "The word is appreciate Mary, you will be careful won't you lass. He is a man of the world, and the newspapers and magazines are full of his experiences. You have seen the women he often appears with so just be careful, I wouldn't want you to get hurt"

Turning worried eyes on Mary, Mrs Grant asked her "Mary did you ask him who the woman was?"

It was the tone in Mrs Grant's voice that caught Mary's attention.

"Yes I did and he said she was just a business associate, a friend, like you are to me. She helps him out in his business sometimes"

At the look of contrite on Mrs Grant, Mary said smugly "He acted like a gentleman all evening, with no touchy feely stuff, I don't think he would hurt me, he said I was a lady, how about that?"

Laughing at the expression on her bosses face, Mary patted her knobbly hand, "I will be careful Pammy, now can I please have a longer lunch today, and can I use the phone to call him and accept his offer for lunch?"

Nodding, Mrs Grant said "Of course you can, you don't have to ask. It's not like that airhead Sandy who calls her boyfriends all the time; you should get yourself a mobile phone"

"Ah, no thanks they are way too expensive and I wouldn't know how to use one, anyway I don't like them" As the elderly lady returned to the front counter her face creased in worry she heard the bell tinkle at the front door to announce a customer.

Letting her mind drift to last night again, Mary knew she had started out being nervous, but he soon put her at ease, making her feel more comfortable with him as the evening got under way.

What surprised her most was when he took her home and gave her a gentle kiss on the lips, Mary found herself leaning into his body, wanting more than a peck, wishing he would kiss her properly, blushing as she remembered feeling his erection as she pressed closer to him.

Was she letting her need to be loved by someone influence her actions, perhaps into letting her shield down? He had been the perfect gentleman all evening showing his upbringing had been exemplary. His parents should be so proud of him, knowing they had a son with perfect manners and consideration for the wellbeing of other people.

Mary wondered about his parents, were they good parents to both the boys as they grew up? Were they always there for them? Did they comfort them when they got hurt? Did they show their love to their sons?

# Chapter 11

Now, for the first time in her memory since she started working, she couldn't wait for it to be the lunch hour. It took her no time at all to rip through the only two orders required for that morning.

Washing her hands at the sink Mary saw her reflection in the mirror; her eyes were shining, her cheeks had a rosy hue, and yes she was excited to be seeing Raoul again.

She finger combed her unruly hair into a high ponytail speculating if Raoul felt the same excitement. Then laughing at her silliness she pocked her tongue out, straightening her shirt and smoothing her skirt with trembling hands.

Mary heard the shop bell again, then Mrs Grant sang out "Mary, Mr Lafette is here" Closing the door to the wet room Mary appeared flustered when she encountered Raoul's possessive gaze.

"You alright girl, you look a bit flushed in the face?" Shrugging her shoulders, Mary said "I'm fine, it was warm in the back room and I was rushing to get the orders finished"

Smiling, she said "I won't be late back Pammy" She knew why she was blushing; it was the thought of being with Raoul again.

No one was more surprised than her that she allowed a man to make her feel … excited, was that the right word? Yes it suited her emotions right down to the ground.

Her friend was talking to Raoul "You have a mind now Mr Lafette, and don't go causing my Mary any upset, she's a very special girl. Remember it's just lunch, right?"

"I will handle her with kid gloves …"

Mrs Grant walked right up to Raoul and into his personal space, and said in a loud whisper right in his handsome face "No you won't, you will keep your kid gloves to yourself sir, or you will answer to me, now off you go and have a nice lunch"

Mary, embarrassed by her friend's words, lowered her flushed face and quickly left the shop. Raoul nodded to the big woman and followed Mary out, a sheepish grin on his face.

"Well she certainly has a way of putting me in my place doesn't she, but you should be happy to have someone caring for you?"

He had a small surprise for Mary for lunch; at least he hoped it would be a nice one. Holding her hand, he led her to his car and held the door for her, happy that she had not kicked up a fuss.

"Where are we going, remember I only have an hour for lunch?" He watched as she settled herself comfortably in his car holding his breath as her skirt rolled up revealing a thigh.

Smiling stiffly he answered "Wait and see, I hope you will like it?" Realising she wouldn't get any more from information from the hard set of his jaw, she sat with her hands on her lap, fingers threaded through each other, showing a small bit of tension.

His glanced at her stiffness, reaching across he held her clenched hands for a moment, then kissed her lips gently "Relax my sweet Mary; I will have you back to work on time"

She smiled when he kissed her and called her 'His sweet Mary'

Looking at the confident way he handled the sports car, his hands almost caressing the steering wheel, a satisfied smile on his face, she could see he loved driving.

"Raoul I must thank you for the gift you sent. A box from Paris sent me into untold excitement, and then to find my favourite tea inside was a brilliant touch, thank you"

He leaned over and patted her hand, never taking his eyes from the road. He appreciated her honesty with his gift, small as it was it had pleased her.

"It was just a small gift Mary, it's not like the new wardrobe or cars I would give my other women, as I said it's no big deal"

Mary thought 'There he goes again, shoving his harem in my face'

Realising he had made a huge blunder; he kept silent until reaching his destination. After about ten minutes, he parked and helped her from the vehicle, moving to the back of the car he removed a basket.

Drawing a sharp breathe, he pointed to the park then held her hand, gently propelling her in saying "We are going to have a picnic, my friend" At the delightful expression on her face, he let out a sigh of relief, then laughed out loud, loving that she could make him feel so carefree.

What was there not to like about the day, he had a beautiful girl for company, the sun was shining although the weather was definitely cool, and for the first time in ages he felt relaxed.

Spreading a rug on the grass, he started to lay out the food which the chef at the Mandarin had made for him. "Oh my goodness Raoul, I have never had a picnic before" His eyes disbelieving as he looked at her, of course she had been on a picnic.

Her eyes were shining.

Yes, he thought, anything was worth it

to see her so happy, and vowed to give her more surprises in the future.

"What do you mean you have never been on a picnic, everyone has been on a picnic at some time when they were growing up?"

Mary lowered her eyes; she was unknowingly telling this man her secrets. Filling her plate with delicious food and then said quietly "Not me, anyway where are we Raoul, I think I recognise this place?"

Laying the bottle of wine aside, frowning he said "Why not you Mary, did not your parent give you that treat?"

Shaking her head Mary thought 'How did you answer such a question when the person asking it had been brought up in the circle of love of both parents'?

Not like her, by being raised in charity, or by threats, or enforced hunger, or beatings, how to answer such an innocent question.

Shaking his head at her silence, he replied "We are in Barnard Park, a great adventure place for children, I thought seeing as you had limited time, we could have lunch near your work"

"Ah yes, I sometimes walked through

here in the summer when I first worked for Mrs Grant, but I haven't done it for a long while. Too busy in the shop as Mrs Grant can't do the things she used to do anymore"

Smiling, he asked "So this was a good idea yes, and have I given you pleasure little one, oui" Mary fiddled with a crisp white serviette, refusing to look at him, her cheeks in full bloom "Oh my goodness yes, it was very thoughtful of you."

They talked for a while about her wanting to learn more about landscaping and other things. Then she startled him by saying dreamily "I would also like to design gardens, as I told you I like mucking around in the dirt"

Looking at all the fare spread before her she hesitantly asked "Is this the kind of food people usually have at picnics Raoul, there seems to be an awful lot just for two people?"

Passing her a crystal glass filled with white wine, he shrugged his magnificent shoulders. "I was not sure of what your tastes were Mary so I had my chef fix a variety for you" Savouring the wine, she wasn't sure, but it tasted like the one she had on their last dinner date. Frowning, had she heard him right?

He had a chef to cook for him?

Stunned at the matter of fact attitude he had about having a personal chef; she knew she was way out of her comfort zone.

He must be very rich to have a private chef, so what was she doing going out with this man who appeared to have everything.

That was the question going round and round in her head, and she realised she wanted answers.

She was just a flower shop girl, with no past, well … with a murky past that she could just about remember from the age of seven, but it was a sordid story he would not like to hear about.

So why did he want her in his life, was it just about lust, she dredged her mind back having read about that when she visited the local library, and feeling stupid about blushing at some of the explicit pictures.

Blimey, it was only a flipping book, but could she really permit a man do some of these things to her body. Looking at Raoul, Mary knew yes, if it was him. It was time for her to take charge of her emotions and not let her sad past deprive her of a future, of possible pleasure, of happiness.

Maybe even a home.

A family

Yes, he was just the man to help her. She knew he wanted her, hadn't he said as much.

Coming out of her revere, she swallowed a mouthful of food that tasted like sawdust now; Mary nervously said "You have a chef Raoul?" Something in her voice made him look at her. He realised she was wary.

Why, because he had a personal chef?

Oh for goodness sake, he was not ashamed of having money; he had earned it through sheer bloody hard work and good intelligent investments.

Trying to put her at ease, he grinned "Do you like the wine it is the same one we had last evening? I asked it to be included in the hamper. To answer your enquiry, I do not have a private chef per se; he is a friend and a chef at the French restaurant I frequent and he will occasionally cook for me. He was kind enough to arrange this food, why, does it not appeal to you?"

He could see the anguish in her eyes, and wondered what caused it. Was it because he had made a slip of mentioning having a private chef? Was it because she thought he was *too* rich?

Watching her carefully pack the remains of their lunch he felt suddenly … perturbed.

"Mary, what is wrong? Did I say something to cause you to feel uncomfortable?" He saw her gaze slip away from him, the tension in the air was so thick you could have cut through it with a knife.

As she tried to fit the remains of the food into the picnic basket avoiding his eyes, he made a sudden decision. Moving forwards, Raoul crouched down next to her and caught her hands with his strong fingers.

"Please Cherie; explain to me what I have done? What has caused you this distress you show on your beautiful face? You must be frank with me; I would walk on hot coals before I intentionally hurt you. Now talk to me"

"Oh Raoul you haven't hurt me in any way, it's just I don't come from your world, jeez, you have your own chef for goodness sake and a family vineyard"

The relief he felt was shown in his laughter. "Is that all, Mon Dieu, I thought it was something serious. As I said he is a friend first and foremost. The extra plus is he is also a three star Michelin trained chef, and I would love him to come and work for me in Singapore, unfortunately he is stubborn and wishes to stay in the U.K, Mary are you a snob?"

Mary stilled, not understanding his question, why would Raoul think she was a snob "What, how dare you why would you think that of me?"

He raised his eyebrows, "Because you are constantly questioning me about my assets. I meant no insult to you my sweet girl. Yes I have money, but I work hard for it, I also employ thousands of staff in various places of work, yes I have the luxuries of life because they go with my life-style and the people I do business with would expect nothing less than the best hence a personal chef."

Oh boy this was a day for revelations.

Her beautiful green eyes flew to his face "You work in Singapore, but I thought you worked here in London?"

Raoul shook his head his gorgeous dark hair lifting in the breeze. God this woman was full of questions. "Yes Mary, my Head office is based in Singapore, in Orchard Road near the Ion building, do you know anything about Singapore?"

He knew she didn't, so her negative response wasn't unexpected. Did he really need to go to all this trouble just to get her into his bed?

Yes he did, because his lust knew no bounds where this woman was concerned.

"I have never been outside of England Raoul; I don't know anything about Singapore"

He needed to watch what he said when talking to her, not be as open about his assets just yet as he felt her pulling away from him.

"My lovely Mary, that will change, I want to show you my world, to be comfortable in it. I promise to be your guide in this new adventure. I will be by your side in every part of your discovering the joys of different foreign travel"

His voice was husky, thick with emotion as he delivered this promise. Raoul's touch was an aphrodisiac when he ran finger down her cheek, and she craved more.

# Chapter 12

His finger left her face and caressed her rosebud lips. Leaning towards her, he ran his tongue along her bottom lip until she opened to him like a flower opening her petals to the heat of the sun.

When he kissed her lips she hesitantly accepted it, he pressed his mouth harder.

It was electrifying; it was like breathing oxygen into his tired soul.

Plunging his tongue into her moist interior, he felt her tongue tentatively touch his, she tasted of innocence, and lust immediately bust into every part of his frustrated body.

He was in paradise.

How to continue this without frightening her had him thinking. Of course, soft French words always worked.

Gently pushing her back onto the rug he took his fill of her exquisite mouth. All sensibility went out the window. He spoke loving words of French, knowing she could not understand him, at least he hoped not, but Mary had to be his, now.

His brain had disappeared; he was in total sexual freefall, and desperately all he wanted to do was touch *her*, not through her clothes, but her soft skin.

His hands were unsteady as he buried them under her shirt, and felt her glorious breasts through her cheap bra.

Pulling her bra out of the way, he exposed them to his hungry eyes, his hand sought the softness of her, and her nipples pebbled instantly, demanding. He had to have them in his empty mouth.

Her nipples were hard in his mouth and he felt he could suckle on them forever.

Was that him moaning, if it was he couldn't have cared? He had … no needed to taste her again. He bent down to suckle on the other one. Oh yes, the taste of her was ambrosia and he craved more, so much more.

Lost in the rush of the sensations whirling through his body for her, he knew he had never experienced this with any other woman; the unique taste of her was food to his starving body and he would satisfy that yearning *now.*

Why he has waited so long he would never know.

He was Raoul Lafette, and he had never waited to bed any woman in his life, his pain was excruciating from the pressure behind his trouser zip, he had to relieve it now.

He threw his leg over her body as he pressed his swollen erection into her, then his brain sluggishly kicked into gear, registering something.

The noise of children shouting and laughing. Children Mon Dieu, what the hell, breathing heavily he surged to his feet, trying to gain some control, and turned away from her so she could not see the bulge in his bespoke trousers.

Wiping a shaking hand across his brow, he berated himself. Merde, he was all ready to take her, on the ground, and in the park.

Thank God the children's voices penetrated his foggy brain. He already knew he had to treat Mary gently or she would flee. And what did he do, he well-nigh had sex in the open with her.

He was losing his equilibrium with this woman.

When Raoul had his body under tight control, he put out a hand to help her up "Come Mon Amie, it's time for you to return to work, I apologise for keeping you out so long, I do not want to face Mrs Grant's wrath again"

Taking a deep breath he tried to soften his tone when he realized how hard it had been. He tried to smile but it was a poor effort, he had wanted her so badly, and knew he needed to cool down, rapidly.

Mary's face was red with embarrassment, realising she had had her fingers firmly spread through his slightly long gorgeous thick hair, while he had been caressing her breasts, and she had moved sensuously against the hard ridge pressing into her stomach.

Appalled, she quickly turned away to fix her bra as he surged to his feet, and he moved away from her … in disgust?

A moment later she grasped his extended hand and he raised her off the ground. Continuing to straighten her clothes with trembling fingers, Mary watched as he lifted the hamper and moved away to stowed it in the boot of his car then he turned holding the door open for her.

Cursing that he had let his emotions get in the way.

Walking to the car on rubbery legs, Mary was horrified at the length she had allowed Raoul to go, not only that but she had enjoyed his attention. What an idiot she was, as his actions proved he had just sex on his mind.

Sitting beside him, she was very tense, her fingers twisted in anguish, she had so looked forward to seeing him again.

When he walked her to the shop door, he reached for her hand; it looked so small enveloped in his large one. "Mary, do not be afraid of me, I long to see more of you, we have such strong feelings for each other, please tell me you feel it also. I know I overstep myself in the park? Will you forgive me my angel, if I ask pretty please?"

His dimple appeared giving his smile a magic image, like the sun coming out to shine on her and fill her up with warmth.

How could she go back to being untouched when she could still feel his need pressed against her, the thrill of his mouth suckling her like a baby, no not a baby, like a lover, while she enjoyed every moment of him touching her, already waiting for the next time he would bring her body alive.

Mary now knew she had become besotted with this man. Drowning in his yummy brown eyes, then just for a moment she thought she saw a flicker of … was that anxiety?

His tongue popped out to touch his top lip. She noticed he did this unthinkingly, more when he was concentrating.

"I don't know what I did wrong but you have no need to say sorry to me. I know I mucked up somewhere by the way you turned away from me in disgust. I don't understand why I feel this way with you, because I don't like men ..." Raoul quickly kissed the words away, his mouth calming her harsh words.

Oh it was nectar kissing her, and he wanted more.

He reached behind her and opened the door "No Mary, *you* did nothing wrong, and I most certainly was not repulsed by you, but I was embarrassed that I had nearly lost control, and did not want you to see how much my body yearns for you. Don't get me wrong Mary, I want you like I want oxygen, and until I bed you I will constantly walk around with this want in my body until your mine"

Nodding to the shop window Raoul was looking through he told Mary "By the looks of the line of customers in the shop I suspect Mrs Grant may be in need of a bit of help. We will talk later my sweet one, please do not be afraid of me as I will guard your life with my own my sweet angel, can we meet again on Sat morning please?"

Kissing her again quickly when Mary

agreed, entering the shop Mary hugged herself, Raoul said she did nothing wrong and he wanted to see her again this coming Saturday. It couldn't come quick enough for her.

She was being really strong wasn't she, letting him touch her, kiss her, fondle her. She let a man touch her and she hadn't cringed away. Punching the air in triumph with a silent YES, she entered the shop.

Helping Mrs Grant who was busy at the counter serving a customer while more were waiting to be attended to, her friend wasn't blind to the bloom of awakening in her protégée's eyes, and worried for her.

Before locking up for the night Mrs Grant informed Mary she had employed another person to help in the shop, which was great news, as that would help take some of the stress off Mary's shoulders.

Later that evening Raoul phoned her as she climbed into bed, they had a lovely talk about everything and nothing about the weather here in London, about how long she studied for her certificate in floristry, he even told her something about his work in

Singapore, she could hear in his voice the respect he had for that lovely country.

Mary longed to put a gift in her box of memories of the events of her outing, but how do you capture a kiss, a feeling? Sleep came easy to her that night, with no nightmares.

Friday night Raoul phoned Mary and cancelled their arrangement for Saturday, saying he had to go out of town early for an important business meeting.

The disappointment she felt was … unexpectedly painful.

Why painful? Then she remembered the conversation with him on the phone.

When she asked him if he had to break their date because of work, he became cold, saying his work was the most important thing in his life. He would discuss it with her if and when he returned.

Well she had been told off in no uncertain terms, serves her right for being nosey. Thinking how cold he had been to her made for restlessness throughout the day.

Usually the shop was extra busy on Saturday and thank goodness it kept her mind off her disappointment. Also the new girl Lily was a great help.

Mary had a phone call from David Holt inviting her for afternoon tea; he said he had a request from another hotel wanting her shop to arrange a display for their foyer.

Mrs Grant was overjoyed at the chance to add another hotel to her small growing list, and she knew it was thanks to Mary's diligence in her preparations for perfection the floral arrangements she offered the clients.

An early request came in for a special bouquet to be delivered to a new mother at the Private Maternity Care Hospital for a favourite customer, Mrs Grant asked Mary to deliver the flowers on her way to the meeting with David.

Arriving at the hospital in the busy lunch hour, Mary found a rare parking spot across the road from the hospital entrance in front of the take-away café.

How unusual because that particular street was always full of trucks doing deliveries, but she was quick to grab the empty space.

Smiling at her audacity she got out of the van and waved a sorry to the other driver who was hoping to snatch the spot. Closing the back door of the van, Mary noticed a very smart long black limousine illegally parked right in the front entrance, the chauffer in the driver's seat.

Hmm Mary wondered, 'Where have I seen that car before, so if you have money to can get away with illegal parking.' Gently holding the sweet smelling flowers with a pink balloon floating from the centre with congratulations printed on it, she made her way across the road, eyeing the vehicle and headed to the front desk, and left them with the receptionist.

After making a quick dash to the ladies, Mary swung the door wide and was surprised to see Raoul leading a pregnant woman down the corridor; he stopped to kiss her tenderly on the mouth, his hand stroking the woman's stomach then hold her to his muscular body ... intimately.

It was the same redhead ... Mary thought 'So I was right she was pregnant, but why was Raoul with her?

Mary immediately felt pain, oh not physical pain, but a bad jolt to her heart.

So this was his urgent out of town business, she should have known better.

Raoul and his companion left the hospital; he had his arm around the woman and helped her into the limousine. Stopping for a moment to talk to the driver Raoul noticed Mary watching him from across the road, and she did not look happy, in fact she was very angry.

Damn and blast.

— ❀ —

Meeting David at the little café near the building of the proposed new job, he was a very engaging companion. He could see she was disturbed about something so he kept the discussion on plants and arrangements to hold her attention. After a while Mary concentrated on him and stopped thinking about Raoul, and his lying to her.

It appears David is an avid gardener and has a small plot near his flat, which he enjoys when he isn't working. He offered to show her one day … if she wasn't too busy.

"Thank you David, I would love to put you right about some of your methods concerning gardening"

Laughing at the shocked expression on his face, he soon found his voice "Okay Miss know-all you're on, you name the time and day and I'll make you eat your words"

An idea jumped into Mary's head about introducing David to her gardens in Norfolk, he would love it. The house had enough spare rooms to accommodate him. Hmm

The new job required Mrs Grant approval so Mary said she would be in touch.

It had been a very enjoyable afternoon Mary realised, she hadn't thought once about Raoul.

Then the memory of his cheating and lies came back thick and fast.

Mary was kept busy after arriving back at the shop, as they had received four more phone orders for an assembly of various presentation bouquets, one for a special seventh wedding anniversary from grandchildren to their beloved grandparents, and the customers were picking them up before closing.

Mrs Grant saw the change in her friend the moment she returned to work, but she kept her own council, Mary would tell her what was wrong in her own time.

Meanwhile she listened to Mary explain the job from David Holt and was only too happy to score another floral engagement from a different hotel.

Word was definitely getting out about her shop.

As she worked on the anniversary flowers Mary wondered what kept two people together for seventy years. Was it a secret only a husband and wife shared? Could it be their longevity, or their trust in each other?

Or was it love?

In her heart of hearts that's what was she searching for … love.

# Chapter 13

Seeing Raoul with the woman he said was just a business associate, kissing her and caressing her like an intimate lover upset her, and the fact he'd lied to her.

Again

Was she putting too much importance on Raoul's friendship?

No, she didn't think so because he had made it very clear to her that he wanted to go further into this friendship. He was the one doing the pursuing, seeking her company, he was the one sending her gifts and giving her expensive dinners.

So why was he lying to her, up till now she had known only aloneness in her heart, love was something she longed for but would she ever achieve it, or recognise it, or was it just for other people? Oh, she had Pamela Grant as a very close friend, and some of the people at Rainbow Gardens as friends. Was she asking too much of the Deity to say she wanted a special person just for her. Maybe she could add David to her small group of friends

Then out of the blue she would get the feeling there was a special person for her and she knew in her heart it was not David?

It was almost as though there was someone beside her when she knew there wasn't. Was it her imagination, no, it was unquestionably a strong feeling?

A gentle smile curved her lips at the crazy thoughts, after all who in their right mind would want a screwed-up woman like her, obviously not Raoul not by the looks of things, not when he was still escorting another woman around.

A pregnant woman at that, stuff it to hell, she needed to get her mind off that woman. Except while she worked, her mind kept returning to the picnic lunch date with Raoul, and how she felt when he touched her, and receiving her first proper adult kiss, fanning her hot face with a piece of cardboard, God; he was very good at kissing.

Her emotions were all topsy-turvey at the moment after the incident at the hospital.

So why, for the first time in her life did she want a man to like her? Why did this particular man make her happy? A happy smile broke through her thoughts when she recounted what took place in the park.

Mary knew she'd jumped the gun at her suspicions that he had gone cold on her, perhaps it had been the noise of the children that had caused his sudden withdrawal but his actions were so obvious and proved the opposite in fact.

Then uncertain doubts crowded her mind once more and her fears turned to his reputation with other women, like the red head she saw him with.

Once again, the same woman, there she goes on again about that woman.

Ok so she was gorgeous, tall svelte and all over him like a rash, then what about the women in the social columns of the newspapers and magazines that seemed to be a part of his enjoyment, as he always appeared to hold those women as intimately as he held the redhead.

Was she a part of his social group as well? No she meant more to him even though she was pregnant?

Yea, I bet a friend with benefits.

Whew, she was getting headachy just thinking about that woman. It gave her a sliver of anxiety … or jealousy?

She hoped he wasn't awakening a sensual emotion in her that she couldn't control.

Then she reminded herself, the benefit of the doubt Mary, give the guy the benefit of the doubt. Then she thought not bloody likely, he had lied to her especially when she told him she hated liars.

He was toast.

--------- ❋ ---------

Thinking about his conversation with Mary in the park, Raoul knew he had to be careful in reference to his wealth. Later when she was more secure in their relationship, he would gradually tell her about the Lafette vast businesses.

*Mon Dieu* how close had he come to seducing her and his body was *still* unfulfilled.

Okay, he knew if he lifted his little finger he could have a woman in his bed instantly, or as the old French saying goes *tout de Suite.*

Could he last that long without sex?

Of course he could and he would, he wanted Mary and he would have her. It would take patience and careful planning.

He *was* in control of his body … wasn't he?

Alas his patience was becoming strained by the minute and the more cold showers he had the more impatient he was.

Remembering the day Mary had seen him at the hotel with the luscious Leslie had been a shock to Raoul. At the time it never entered his head that Mary would be the one to do the floral arrangement for his apartment, he thought maybe Mrs Grant would do it, but now he knew more of her work, it made sense it would be her.

The flowers were to cheer Leslie up as she was going to stay at his penthouse after having some important surgery done concerning the success of her IVF treatment. It was the least he could do as he had forgotten their date for the fashion show. He needed to keep in her good books, because she always went over and above for him.

Arriving at his home in Grosvenor Crescent after leaving Mary, Raoul's cell beeped alerting him to a text. Damn and blast, reading the message from his lawyer Raoul had no option; he had to get back to Singapore ASAP. One of the companies he was on the point of finally securing had got cold feet and wanted to renegotiate the deal.

Cancelling another appointment to meet up with his brother in Paris, Raoul called for his private jet to be readied for the early flight to Singapore.

A quick call to let Mary know he had to cancel their arrangements, explaining he had a very important business meeting.

When Mary had asked why, he abruptly

reacted to her questioning him and snapped back angrily "Are you questioning my work ethics, because if you are let me tell you, nothing gets between me and my work, please remember that in the future, we will continue this conversation at a later date, goodbye?"

Damn he didn't have to sound like a bear with a sore...head, excuse the pun.

Stopping off to collect Leslie from the penthouse as promised because she was required to undergo another scan at the Private hospital, then he would be dropped off at the airport while she took his car back to the apartment.

Except it didn't quite work out that way as he saw Mary standing beside her van across the street watching them and she was not happy.

Arriving at Stanstead airport in time for take-off, Raoul had been shocked when he saw Mary. How would he explain his presence in the company of the woman Mary was bound to recognise.

That was a problem he did not have time to solve at the moment, he had to concentrate on the business at hand. Thirty six gruelling hours later Raoul watched his associate hand the completed contract to his legal team and then breathed a sigh of satisfaction.

Raoul grinned like the legendary Cheshire cat, if he wanted something he went after it until it was his. No way was he going to lose out on this lucrative deal; he had put his heart and soul into it for twenty eight months.

Now he could concentrate on his next project, the next big thing he needed to fix … Mary.

He had to clarify his presence at the hospital with Leslie he knew he had been overly affectionate because of her delicate condition which Mary had seen, also to explain why he had not been on his way overseas as he informed her.

———— ❋ ————

Mary was unsettled after her talk with Raoul, he sounded really angry, and she should have kept her mouth shut. So what if he had to go away again on business, she had no right to question him.

Except his business included the red headed woman he appeared with frequently … his associate he called her, but Mary had always doubted that title?

Mrs Grant and Mary went down to Norfolk to inspect the renovations being carried out in the old kitchen. The new helper in the shop, Lily, was proving to be worth every penny she earned. Mrs Grant couldn't be more pleased with the lady.

Lily could even handle the lazy Sandy, who was getting slacker, muddling orders, and arriving late for work. Mrs Grant knew it was time to let her go. There were always more eager girls willing to learn the flower trade.

Plus she was still waiting for Mary to tell her what happened at the hospital.

The new kitchen looked absolutely grand. The old slate floor had been professionally scrubbed; the old wall cabinets and the wooden hutch were stained to have the stressed look to match the huge farmhouse table that could seat ten at a pinch. The sink was replaced with a traditional Belfast one, lovely and deep.

In pride of place sat the state-of-the-art six burner wood and gas cooker. Mary couldn't wait to practice her cooking skills which were sadly neglected in London.

Setting the kitchen to rights gave Mary time to think about Raoul; even though he was a proven womanizer, she missed him. My God, was her self-esteem that fickle, that she would dismiss his actions? Considering it wasn't the first time he lied to her.

He promised her he was not in a relationship with anyone, yet she had seen him with the same woman three times. Her butterflies in her stomach were not happy, no dancing this time, when she thought of Raoul; in fact they had gone to sleep.

Later that night, sitting in front of the huge fire, Mary with a cup of Earl Grey tea, and Pammy with a small sherry, she told her friend about seeing Raoul at the hospital and how it had upset her. Her advice was to wait and let him explain why he lied to her again and not to jump to conclusions.

Although Mrs Grant was happy

that Mary had a new friend in David …
hopefully.

It was late the next evening when Mary
returned to Islington; Pamela decided to
stay in Norfolk for a few more days. Her
breath showing a faint mist as she breathed
out, it was definitely getting colder.

Preparing to close the shop the
following night, Mary is surprised when
Raoul showed up, and caught her around
the waist, lifting her in his strong muscled
arms, the tone of his voice soft and sexy.

"Hello my Mary, Mon Dieu I have missed
you. I have just returned from Singapore,
will you take pity on a starving man. Please
Mary; I need your company tonight?"

Mary decided to take her friends advice.

"Why Raoul your home again, how nice,
sorry I forgot this isn't your home anyway,
it's nice to see you; dinner would be nice
thank you. Do I need to change my clothes
or is this skirt and top ok?" Raoul screwed
his face at the repeated *nice words*.

Right, by the sound of her off hand
greeting he had some crawling to do.

# Chapter 14

Mary was hoping for a quiet moment with him to set him right about how he got the wrong impression that she had questioned him about his work, also she had to know why he broke his date with her, but he was with another woman.

She looked at her work outfit, then away. Okay, she didn't have the money to splurge on clothes; he would just have to take her as is.

Bending down he went to kiss her, but she stepped back a pace, so it landed on her cheek

Not caring that she was blushing beetroot red at her action, Mary enquired coldly "So, where are we eating if you're starving, it can't be a flashy restaurant you know?"

Hearing the distance in her voice, upset him, but what did he expect, that she would drop into his eager arms.

'No,' he thought. Raoul interrupted her with a quick "Did I say I was starving for food? I missed you so much Mary, I pushed as hard as I dare to get through my business, please let me hug you"

His eyes had gone a deep brown; he couldn't get enough of her, as his hands caressed her stiff body, dragging her close to caress her ample hips and so she could feel his need, his damn erection that never seemed to go down around her.

"I need to kiss you my sweet Mary" His French accent thick with longing as he lowered his head, and his tongue played with her lower lip, enjoying the fullness, dragging it into his mouth.

Oh yes the taste of her was intoxicating, and he wanted to put his tongue in a more erotic place, to taste her essence, her womanhood.

It took all his strength just to stay with a kiss.

And halleluiah, she didn't refuse him.

There was no alarm, no fear at him touching her, and she so wanted to run her fingers through his hair, but kept her hands at her side.

Then abruptly she was free.

"I must not let my need for you control this situation, my Mary" he said as he led her to his very conspicuous sports car. Reaching across her to make sure her seat belt was in place, he accidently brushed against her full breast.

Their eyes met, hers cool, his hot with longing, and he kissed her again, only not so gentle this time, and this time he felt her relax, so he let his tongue slide smoothly into her parted lips.

Oh Mon Dieu, she was liquid sunshine, he drank greedily from her mouth, but this was not the place or time.

Raoul was very pleased she is getting used to him touching her. Driving swiftly through the busy evening traffic, he was impatient to get her to his place, but for some reason he did not take her to his home. This was not the time to reveal that sort of information; too much might overload his chances as she was already questioning his wealth.

Pulling into the underground parking of the Mayfair apartment his exit from the car was very elegant, while she struggled from her very low position.

Seeing her predicament he instantly became the gentleman and reached down to help her from the low slung seat.

"Good job you're here to help me or it would have been a much more undignified exit for me. Your car is very low to the ground. How do you manage with your six feet something body getting in and out all the time?"

Laughing at the image she portrayed, "I am used to it, and if it causes you difficulty I will use the limo next time. I was in a hurry to see you and as I had an afternoon flight I left my car at the airport"

Mary knew he was lying as he had been at the hospital.

He saw Mary shake her head in his

peripheral vision; turning to look at her he said "What's wrong Ma Cheri?"

"That can't be right, when you cancelled our date, you said you had a very early take-off, but we know that's not right don't we."

This was not the time to answer this discussion, so when they entered the lift his lack of control took over and he pushed her against the wall, taking her in his arms, burying his face in the softness of her neck, kissing her throat.

He loved the feel of her; he could listen all day to the gentle moans she made when he caressed her. He nibbled at her ear then gave it a slight nip. Hearing her inhale, he kissed her deeply.

He had been contemplating asking her to move in with him, but then something hit him like an express train.

He loved this woman, and yes he had some explaining to do, he had to clear her suspicions of him.

No, no and no, he didn't do love. It was not in the structure of his life. Absolutely not, the longest relationship he had was with Camille, and that was now over, thank

God, he was in enough trouble with this woman.

Mon Dieu the 'Love' word lit up his brain like a firecracker. No way was he given credence to that word. That was a big no-no.

He like the way his life was as a single man. There was not a woman on this planet he would permit to curb his freedom.

Except the need for her to be in his life was so strong it overpowered all his prejudices about marriage.

Whoa, when the hell did marriage come into the equation, he'd just had the word *love* explode in his head, now *marriage?*

He looked at the lovely woman in his arms and thought of her with some other man. Hypothetically shaking his head again, no way; the thought of his lovely Mary with another man was abhorrent to him. She belonged to him and he was not letting her go, so marriage, swallowing the word it would be. He felt totally possessive of her. Damn she was his ... wasn't she?

Yes of course she was his, but was it love, or lust? No he knew lust, what he did not recognise was his unquestionable *need* for this woman.

Trying to clear his head of these troubling thoughts he watched Mary's hips sway as she moved forward out of the lift, and his hands automatically reached for her, to touch her again.

God he had it bad.

Glancing back over her shoulder at him as he pulled her closer to his aroused body and sighed, she was exquisite the way she filled his arms, filled his heart to the exclusion of common sense. His desire to touch her bare skin overcame that common sense and set him on fire.

Mary smiled when he slipped his hand under the tee to caress one of her taut nipples, her breast swelling through her brassiere.

She moaned softly then turned, her arms going round his waist under his designer jacket, holding him tightly, and her voluptuous breasts pressing into his hard body. Then she stood on tip-toes and ran her tongue along his ridged jaw, then his oh so inviting lips.

Mary had voluntarily given her first kiss to a man.

It was like drinking at the forbidden well of love as she deepened the kiss. Mary felt it all the way through her body.

She pressed her thighs together, her need strong for him, for this man she now knew she had no fear of. The joy at discovering a passion for Raoul shocked her.

Then out of the blue her fear raised its ugly head and she pushed away from him, her joy at discovering such a strong longing for a man alarming her.

She would be strong; she would not let her fear destroy this new emotion, this craving for Raoul.

Heat suffused her cheeks as bewilderment shone in her eyes that she raised to him. "I … oh wow, *I* just kissed you, Raoul"

Raoul could hear the tension in her voice as he brushed a wayward strand of hair from her petite face.

"You gave me your first kiss *Mon ange*, please do not apologise because you sent me to heaven, thank you my love."

He could see the bewilderment on her very expressive face so he said softly "As I haven't eaten since this morning we will continue this later, *tu comprends*, now I will order us food, come my darling, tell me what you prefer, you can have anything but I insist no pizzas or Chinese?"

"Seafood would be nice thank you" Mary answered; she loved seafood but rarely indulged because it was too expensive. She was saving every penny for her future dream.

Removing his cell-phone from his discarded jacket but not making the call just yet. He needed a moment to gather his scattered wits. He had to keep a grip on his emotions, how could he call her his 'love' How could his brain tell him he loved her?

This falling in love with this delightful woman was playing havoc with his intelligence? Again the suggestion of love crowded his mind.

So did the word *marriage*. Never in all his years would he allow the thought of marriage to enter the equation, marriage was not for him.

Mary moved further into the apartment, trying to control her shaky breathing, knowing if Raoul had persisted she would have given in to him.

What would he think when he discovered she was a virgin? Would it put him off her? She'd read something about men not liking virgins,

Trying to collect her scattered thoughts, Mary absently surveying the room, not having an arty bone in her body where home decoration was concerned, she saw it still lacked character, or colour.

If he added some bright cushions and maybe pictures it would assuage the starkness, and of course flowers were also a must to bring the room alive.

Sitting down on the red couch she approached the tricky apology she owed him. "Raoul I want to apologise for my cranky attitude when you told me you were going away again, and just now for questioning your mistake. I had no right to say that. Did your business in Singapore go alright?"

Raoul frowned recalling his disquiet

at her questioning his work and about his leaving London.

Meeting Camille for dinner at their favourite restaurant "Paul" in Ngee Ann city had not gone well, and he was right, she was silent for a moment then asked if he had found someone else, he had hated hurting her, but admitted there was someone special now.

All the women he had been involved with knew the rules, so in the end she had accepted, with reluctance, his farewell gift of a diamond necklace which he insisted on putting it round her neck, then kissing her goodbye which she made the most of.

He never bought jewellery for his women, but Camille had been his mistress far longer than any other woman.

Later as he escorted her to his limousine then kissed her goodbye, he didn't see paparazzi in the shadows, the photographer smiled, the photo would go global. All the paparazzi knew Raoul Lafette hated having his privacy invaded, so the woman he dumped deserved her cut.

Bringing his mind back to the question

Mary asked, of course she was talking about his work. So he saw no reason to tell her about Camille as she was his past.

His smile was strained "Yes thanks, but it was touch and go at one stage. In future Mary, do not question my work, as to my flight plan I had to change it for a very special meeting, although you do not need to know what. Now no more mundane talk, I want to know what you have been doing in my absence."

He saw the doubt in her eyes as she replied "But Raoul, I didn't question your work in any shape or form, it was the suddenness of your going away I asked about. One minute you're full of plans for us, then you cancel them as though I wasn't important, then you said you had to leave in the morning, but now you told me you didn't leave until the afternoon, is it any wonder I'm confused."

Leaning back against the soft leather, Mary answered him. "I agree no more talk on that sore subject; you obviously had your reasons to lie to me. I mean it's not as though we are in a serious relationship. Well, what did I do in the time you were away, let me see. I spoke to you umpteen times, and then I did four weddings, two anniversaries, one for a first year of marriage, and another for seventy years. I really enjoyed that one. Then you phoned me again and we chatted. Mrs Grant had hired an older woman to help in the shop and she turned out to be a blessing, it's great because she can handle Sandy and puts her in her place quick-smart, but in a nice way you understand"

Then lifting questioning eyes to him it was all he could do not to smother her with kisses even though he was fuming at her calling him a liar. "Unfortunately I had to make a floral tribute for a family that lost a baby"

He saw her beautiful eyes cloud with unshed tears.

Making an effort to be calm, he sat next to her and wiped a tear that escaped "Do you want children Mary? I mean if you ever married?"

# Chapter 15

For some reason her answer was important to him. Mon Dieu, now he was bringing children into the mix.

Shaking his head a little, what the hell was wrong with him? Was he mad?

Her smile was a lovely sight to see as she answered him "I would love to have a child, to make a family with the man I love, and the man I eventually marry would have to love children also"

Leaning in he lifted her onto his lap with his strong muscular arms, how could he stay angry with this precious woman. Raoul planted little kisses on her forehead, down her small nose, and her chubby cheeks, until his tongue licked her pouting lips.

Mary became compliant in his arms and opened her mouth surrendering to his eager kisses … and he lost it.

This little woman had everything a man could dream of, she was more than a handful to hold and it gave him great satisfaction to know she had finally stopped resisting him. It was like an explosion in his head.

Raoul was stunned by the strength of the emotions he felt for her. He had never even had sex with her, never taken her to bed, but he knew without a doubt he wanted this woman.

He loved her. Finally Raoul admitted it and accepted it, he loved Mary. How had it sneaked past his sensible brain and penetrated his cold heart.

When he was in Singapore he found it hard to concentrate on business. After he ended the affair with Camille, all he thought of was Mary; all he wanted was to talk to her. All he could do was imagine her bountiful body, her soft and inviting lips, as well as her elusive aroma that he reckoned he could sometimes catch a whiff of at unexpected moments.

God he had missed her.

So he worked all hours and drove his staff to breaking point to get back to Mary.

As Mary shifted to sit astride his powerful thighs, her skirt rode high over her hips, her sensible white cotton panties showing as she ground her woman's core against his arousal, he growled "Mary I need you so badly, please let me love you. I can't hold back any longer, you are exquisite and I must taste you."

Oh yes, the bulge in his designer pants told her this was true and surprisingly she wasn't embarrassed.

All she had to do was get the discussion of her virginity out of the way. Granted she had wanted to be married before gifting it to a man. Raoul ran his trembling hand up her legs and felt her soft skin. Laying her down, he inserted one powerful thigh between her legs.

Mary was on cloud nine; taking his head in her small hands she rained light kisses over his face in between laughing. Sucking strongly on his earlobe she had taking into her mouth, flicking it backwards and forwards with her tongue, while his hands were busy touching her.

Should she tell him at this moment in time that she had never been with a man?

How to relax, gosh she didn't know how to relax

When this man touched her as intimately as he was, she must have unconsciously relaxed because she was feeling his strong hands pulling her shirt off and his fingers caressing her skin.

Her nipples were so hard she thanked God when he ended her frustrations and bent his head and took one into his mouth. Trying to supress a moan, Mary snuggled closer to his big powerful body, her hands shaking as she undid the buttons of his shirt.

The sudden need to touch his bare chest was vital, and she gloried in his helping her when he ripped his shirt down the front and buttons went flying everywhere.

Then she felt the bulge in his pants move

and pressing into her wet flesh making her think of … more please.

Oh yes, that felt so good she didn't want him to stop in fact she pressed closer to his touch. Mary was totally lost in the excitement of what was happening to her body that she didn't realise his hand had moved to her knickers, her first thought was…at last.

Raoul knew he had her; she was his he would make this glorious for her.

Now partly lying on her, his torturous erection was so painful that he needed relief *now*. Sliding one hand down from her bountiful breast he gently caressed the silky soft skin of her stomach, down to the elastic at the top of her panties.

Mary was so lost in the enjoyment in what he was doing to her when he began to rub a finger into the damp heart of her.

She thought she could see her shining rainbow in her happiness, and then its abrupt disappearing when she felt a jolt in her heart. Coming to her senses she jerked away from him and pushed at his heavy body, clambering over him she cried in distress.

"Oh my God, no, you have to stop Raoul; please I'm sorry I can't … I didn't mean to … I can't do this"

His brain functioning at minus intelligence, he lifted his lust filled gaze to her, not comprehending for the moment what she was saying when his body was shrieking for satisfaction.

Shaken his head to dispel the fog of desire which was blocking his judgment, it quickly brought him to clarity, then his eyes changed to a cold stare, had he heard right? No, he could not believe it; his frustration was at boiling point.

He had never had a knock-back in his life.

Standing up he adjusted his trousers, his eyes as ice cold as his voice when he questioned her "What did you say? Let me get this straight, are you a tease Mary? Do you do this to all men, or is it just me?"

All the desire he was feeling for her instantly turned off, boy did she know how to deflate a guy. He knew he was being an arrogant ass, but he had wanted … no ached with his last breath to be inside this woman, to feel her warmth, ah just to feel her would be heaven, now nothing.

And she was refusing him? Well no one refused Raoul Lafette without consequences. Come hell or high water he was going to bed this woman. As his shocked attack on her person began to sink in Mary bristled with indignation, and hurt. How dare he call her a flirt, she hadn't ever been this close to a man, and most certainly never let a man touch her so intimately in her life.

Still shaken, the emotions rippling through her body, Mary struggled to retrieve her shirt from the floor and rounded on Raoul, her face consorted with misery but her stance ready for a fight.

Attempting to put her top on, her fingers all thumbs, she felt dismayed that he could attach her, couldn't he see how distressed she was.

Then her anger took over, hands on her hips the action pulling her shirt taut and outlining her very pronounced breasts.

"Hang on; you want to run that past me again, how dare you, you who have had more women than I have had hot dinners, and took relish in boasting about them to me, how dare you to slight my innocence? How cleaver of you to have removed my clothes while you are partially dressed. You have blackness in you Raoul Lafette and you also lied to me when I told you I can't abide liars. I have decided I don't want anything more to do with you. I have never been with a man; I don't do things like this. I don't know how to …"

Stuttering to a stop, pain now filling her heart, her eyes brimming with tears which she fought, and Raoul forgave her immediately. Reeling at what he had just heard, Mon Dieu, a virgin, and he nearly jumped on her like a crass teenager.

A virgin, Raoul tried to dislodge the vision she had put into his head. Never in his life had any of his relationships involved a virgin, well this changed everything.

He would have to handle this situation with kid gloves, but finally the sweet Mary would be his, as he intended to marry her.

Pacing the room in agitation he knew

he had to cool down before he ruined everything.

Wait that was twice she called him a liar, that accusation needed addressing. Raoul turned away at this thought, moving to the floor to ceiling windows. What lie, he racked his brain but came up blank, then he asked himself why he was not more disturbed at the idea of *marriage* but disturbed at her saying he was a liar?

Also hadn't he mentioned children somewhere in a conversation with her? Children, him and children, no way he was definitely losing the plot.

He knew she was really important to him, never in any of his relationships with the other women had his body hungered like it did for her.

She was constantly on his mind, hadn't he proved that with the frequent phone calls to her when he was away on business, something he never did.

He dreamt about her, he missed her, he loved the feel of her; he loved listening to her talk of her beloved flowers and what she was growing in the miniscule garden at the back of the shop.

She was intoxicating.

Conclusion … it was time he settled down and raised a family and Mary was the woman he wanted to do it with. He loved her, so marriage was the obvious next step. No more stalling, it was time for definite action.

Turning round he saw Mary had finished dressing but still angry "I apologise Mary, I withdraw any implication I made on your innocence. Are you telling me you are a virgin, and when did I lie to you?"

"That's none of your damn business mister, now I want to go home, and before you offer, I'll call for a taxi" Shaking his head he slowly moved towards her, taking her hand.

"Ah my sweet Mary, you are magnificent in your anger, I can see I'm going to have a happy and fulfilling life with you as my wife, you will certainly keep me on my toes. Who would have guessed? A virgin, Mary you take my breath away. Now, we will not consummate …"

"Hold up you. What do you mean "as your wife" and stop trying to kiss me; you're an idiot if you think ... mmm, stop"

She muttered, loving the way he nibbled on her swollen lips, trying to resist him, only he didn't stop and her protests gradually diminished into low husky moans of pleasure, as he continued caressing and kissing her, his voice rasping with emotion.

"Oh my sweet girl I could not stop kissing you anymore than I could stop breathing the air I need to survive. I am the biggest fool in creation. I simply got carried away with my need for you. I have been frustrated and carried a permanent erection around since the day I saw you; I have tried so hard to cool my ardour, but you make it difficult for me you beautiful girl"

By this time Mary had stopped struggling against him and stood passive in his arms.

"Please ma Cherie, does not the earth move for you as it does for me, does not the day shine with sunlight, even at night, I beg of you, please do not be angry with me anymore. Surely you too can feel the chemistry between us; I have never had that with any of my past lovers"

This was not what she wanted to hear, and this was not the time to boast about his other conquests.

Stiffening it brought to mind the beautiful woman she saw draped all over him.

Raoul felt her body harden. Merde, why doesn't he think before he opens his big mouth? "That was a stupid remark, please ignore it, you know I am here for only you my darling, but you know I have had other women, and that subject is now closed we will speak of them no more my sweet, you are everything I need" Gently rubbing her arms, he placed little kisses all over her face.

Mary did not know it yet but she would give him the greatest gift a man could receive from a woman, her innocence, her virginity.

His ego was going through a huge boost, and he felt like strutting around. He was so full of pride, to his knowledge he had never deflowered a virgin.

But not this woman, no he would not take her virginity; she was one of a kind.

Mary dislodged his hand from her nape saying in a strangled voice "I really don't want to hear about your other woman, not when you have just asked me to marry you. You did … I mean … propose?" He grasped her hands, kissing the back of them "Yes my love I did Mary, will you do me the honour and be my wife, I promise to make you happy, and protect you. I will never harm you. I will do my upmost to be the best husband and father I can. Under no circumstances will I betray your love. I love you my angel, please Mary what is your answer?"

# Chapter 16

Thrilled and anxious at the same time, Mary could feel hope building inside her as she looked into Raoul's deep brown eyes, and she saw sincerity reflect back at her.

He had promised never to hurt her, so she would lock her anxieties in a steel box and throw away the key because she was willing to give life a try, to change her life with a man.

Wait, did he mention fatherhood but that meant … babies.

It was time for her to leave her fears behind and start living a life of joy, to trust, to come out of the darkness.

It was time for her to find her happy

place in her rainbow and to find her rainbow's end, was it his hand at the end of her rainbow, oh God she hoped so. Feeling her heart pounding as Raoul cradled her body; Mary brought her fingers to scroll up his mighty chest in a gentle exploration. Loving the passion her body was getting from him. Her fingers were tingling as she reached the throbbing pulse at the base of his throat.

The turbulence of unknown emotions sweeping through her as yet sexually unawakened body wasn't enough wasn't satisfying. She only knew she wanted more … no needed more, and only Raoul could give her that fulfilment.

Lifting herself up onto her toes, Mary looked into stormy brown eyes. "Answer me please, will you be my wife?" Raoul pleaded. Her lips barely just touching Mary whispered

"Yes my love I will proudly be your wife"

Then she kissed him, and it was the most erotic kiss he had ever received from a woman. He drank his fill from her innocent mouth, but the fire in his body could not be quenched with only a kiss.

Opening his eyes he saw the blush staining her cheeks and how hard she was breathing then he realized he had her pressed hard against the lounge room wall.

When had he moved? He couldn't remember, but he could see by the rapid pulse in her neck, she was as aroused as he was and desire raced through his body. Plus his damn erection was throbbing and jumping in his pants, trying to escape.

Lifting her slight figure, Raoul rotated his hips so his shaft fitted into her female mound. Closing his eyes he could feel his body building up to an early release.

No, he would not allow his emotions to embarrass him, swiftly pulling away from her, resting his forehead on hers, his breath coming in short bursts; he breathed in deeply to regain his self-control.

Taking her hand, he led her to the hidden bar and pulled out a counter high chair "Sit Mary, Oh my sweet girl I want you so much, but not like this. I also want you to stay innocent until we marry. God, did I just condemn myself to celibacy. How soon can we marry, I beg you not to keep me waiting too long?"

The smile on Mary's face was enough to make him forget all his vows of celibacy, but no, he really and truly wanted Mary to save herself for their wedding night, now that he knew she was untouched.

Placing two frosted champagne flutes before her, he popped the top of a bottle of champagne. Oh boy, he thought, he could just feel the future cold showers he would have to put up with. But Mary was worth it.

Never in his life had he restrained his sexual urges, if he wanted relief, he had it on speed dial, but not anymore.

"No my love I won't keep you waiting long, but we can't marry yet as Christmas is just around the corner, would February be ok with you?"

"Sweetheart I would marry you tomorrow if I could, I will try to be patient, but I warn you I'm not a very patient man where you're concerned, I visualise more cold showers for me for a while"

"Poor boy" Mary felt comfortable

enough now in Raoul's company to crack a joke with him. His cheeks suffused with colour at her jibe.

"Mary I would like you to move in with me. I need to see you every day, and the only way I will achieve that is if you're here with me. I want to hold you in my arms at every opportunity. God it's going to be hard not making love to you, but I will give it my best shot. You can even use the spare bedroom, but please my sweet love, come, live with me"

The look in his eyes showed his need, his love, plus the sincerity in his voice, she liked that, it made her feel like … wanted, loved.

"Raoul we have so much to discuss and I would like to involve Mrs Grant in these arrangements as she has been like a mother to me since I was a young girl. I will come and live with you, but it would not be until after the Christmas festive season, and the New Year. We are rushed off our feet at these important celebrations …"

Moving to her side he interrupted "Thank you my love now drink up, we have a lot to celebrate" Clicking her glass he said softly "To you my love, you have made me a very happy man, I want to take you shopping tomorrow and buy you your engagement ring"

Just as she was about to answer him, he surprised her by hesitating briefly, then unexpected as he said "Now I know we both want children, but can we have the first year just to ourselves, to get to know each other … intimately"

Drowning in the love shinning in her stunning dark green eyes, Raoul tipped her chin up and kissed her with all the love in his heart, and she responded instantly, with no fear, letting him know how much she trusted him and returned that love.

Placing her still nearly full glass down Mary enquired her voice husky with emotion "I haven't seen your entire home Raoul, only the two rooms I used for the floral arrangement, is it all as sterile as this?"

Flummoxed at her words, it took a moment for Raoul to realise she thought he was talking about this apartment.

"Oh my sweet girl, I do not live here, the company use it for visiting dignitaries and business associates and entertaining"

The questioning look in her eyes confused him momentarily, as he was about to answer her, his phone shrilled loudly. Looking at the caller he excused himself, he moved away a little. "Hello Les how's it hanging?"

Laughing, his countenance changed dramatically, a frown on his face as he spoke in rapid French. Watching him as he quickened his stride away from her towards the large windows for more privacy to continued his conversation.

As Raoul spoke in low urgent tones, Mary eyed his virile body and thought how handsome he was; he could have easily made his fortune as a male model.

His physic was hard with rippling muscle, his face hard at times when he was thinking; he also licked his top lip with the tip of his tongue in concentration. His brown eyes darkened when in deep emotion, just like hers. His dark hair just made for fingers to mess with, especially her fingers.

Oh boy, these naughty thoughts kept surprising her, never in her life had she thought like that, but at the moment she had more serious things to think about.

Like if Raoul didn't live here then where did he live, and did he also use this apartment for … what?

Then she remembered, of course he did, hadn't she seen that for herself the day she worked in this very room and the bedroom arranging a flower display at his request for his special lady friend, possibly the lady who's toiletries had been displayed in the bathroom.

Could they belong to the same lady he had told her was only a business associate, the same lady she had seen him with in the lobby that had been draped all over him like creeping ivy, also the same woman at the hospital.

Yes he definitely had some explaining to do concerning his relationship with this woman, but that would need to be a serious discussion for the future, as Mary would not be a third wheel in any man's life. Turning to see Raoul was still in deep conversation with the man he called Les.

Mary wandered around then headed into the master bedroom to use the bathroom. Washing her hands she noticed female items still placed on the top of the vanity unit. Picking up the perfume bottle Mary sniffed, Yuk, recoiling instantly way too strong for her, it would have to be a special woman to wear that heavy fragrance.

Returning to the bedroom Mary is surprised to see Raoul stretched out on the large canopied bed, scrolling through his phone.

Sitting on the edge of the bed Mary asked "All finished with your call Raoul?" Smiling at her, he threw the phone down and lifted her bodily into his arms, brushing her glorious hair away from her face behind her small ears. "Yes my love, now kiss me, it's been a while and I thirst to feel your ripe lush lips quench my need"

Mary was in heaven; Trying to catch her breath as his tongue played with the opening of her mouth then delved into its warmth. She tasted like … sweet wine, no like … a woman, yes that was it.

How he wanted this woman.

# Chapter 17

It had been Leslie on the phone informing him that Ramsey Investigations had found the person who was stealing the designs and was being dealt with as we speak.

Of course Leslie had heard her favourite billionaire's involvement with a lady friend, but why she was causing him lost sleep. "It is confidential so butt out" he told her.

He could hear her laughing, "Okay lover but if it's the same woman we saw at the apartment, be careful as her look of innocence could be a part of her allure that's got your attention, by the by, your picture was in the international papers, very touching, you kissing your mistress, and very naughty of you if your serious about little orphan Annie" Damn why had his PA had not informed him of those photos, he hoped Mary hasn't seen them. "Thanks Les, I owe you one" Laughing she chirped "You Raoul Lafette will owe me a lot more than one"

Raoul had been lied to once before in his younger days by a woman he thought was innocent and loved him until she tried to screw him over for millions.

He knew his Mary was the real thing. In the back of his mind he knew she was not experienced, her innocence showed when he kissed her, she had no idea at first how to respond.

Raoul had no doubt that what you saw in Mary was what you got; she was like an open book. He smiled, oh yes a book he was determined to read and enjoy from cover to cover and under the covers.

His strong arms pinned Mary to the mattress with the help of a muscled thigh, kissing her throat with nibbling small bites, while his hand was busy caressing her breasts. He was as proud as punch of her for getting over her fear of men, so that she trusted him now.

"I could eat you up my darling, you taste so delicious, and how you managed to stay pure is beyond my reasoning, it will take tremendous strength not to make love to you until we marry, but I have promised and I always keep my word"

Flopping onto his back, he brought Mary close "My love, I have unpleasant news for you. I am so sorry but I have to go to Singapore again in the morning, I am needed to deal with an ongoing problem that I thought I had dealt with. I will probably be away for Christmas maybe longer"

Mary gasped, then tried to move away from him, but he held her tight "I know how disappointed you are but look to the future when we will be together for always" Kissing her passionately he then moved off the bed, adjusting his clothes.

Scrambling to her feet Mary was all set to argue when she remembered his reactions the last time, so she kept her mouth shut, after all she would be flat out up to Christmas with orders.

Mrs Grant always tried to give Mary a sense of family tradition, particularly at Christmas. "I am sorry to leave you again so soon my love, but after Christmas I will slow down my work hours to spend quality time with you"

———— ❀ ————

When Raoul dropped her back at her flat he held her for a long moment, rubbing his chin on the top of her head, he appeared distracted then whispered "I am going to miss you my love, please kiss me so I can keep it in my heart until we are together again"

His kiss curled her toes, she hugged him tightly, not wanting to let him go "I already miss you my love, please hurry back to me" As he leaped into his car he blew her a finger kiss which she couldn't see through her tears.

As predicted the shop was flat out over the festive season, thankfully Mary was too busy to think of Raoul, that she literally fell into bed at night, exhausted.

So after Christmas with Raoul gone and Mrs Grant already in Fakenham, Mary closed the London premises at lunch time on Christmas Eve for the three days of the holidays, and then drove down to Norfolk.

Mary loved the slower pace of the festive season in Fakenham; passing through the local village was like a winter's tale, lovely coloured lights in windows and Christmas tress showing off their beautiful old fashioned homes wearing the Holly and Mistletoe as in years gone by.

The large tree that sat in the village green, covered in twinkling lights, dressed in colourful decorations, plus the soft white snow on the leaves looked like a flamboyant silver evening gown, the shop windows full of beautiful exhibits of Christmas stories of bye-gone days.

Mary would laugh as she tried to walk through the flurries of gently fallen snow or watch her breath puff when she exhaled, like a wisp of winter air.

The local people would come to Rainbow

Gardens and Mrs Grant would give them their Christmas foliage, red berries for garlands, holly, wreaths; stop for a while and have a chat while drinking a mug of hot chocolate.

Then they would all congregate to the small church and dress it with the help of the old vicar and his wife. They made a pretend stable depicting the nativity scene every year.

Mary was going to ask Raoul if he wanted to join her this year, then it dawned on her she had never told him about Rainbow Gardens. Why, she hadn't meant to keep it a secret it just never came up in their conversations. Anyway he would not be here for this Christmas, so she would tell him when he returned. It made Mary a bit sad because it would have been their first Christmas together.

——— ❀ ———

It was ten weeks before Raoul returned to London, Mary had heard from him spasmodically when she returned to work after the Xmas break. Then on one of his infrequent calls he told her he had to go from Singapore to New York for a couple of days, but he would be home soon, and she hadn't heard from him since.

Ten weeks, so what was going on?

David Holt had invited her and Mrs Grant to afternoon tea to consult directly about bringing more business their way. At dinner one evening they had ferocious debates about horticulture which they all enjoyed.

David was a frequent visitor to Rainbow Gardens now.

She made frequent calls to Raoul, but he never picked up, she made excuses for him in her head why he refused her calls. He was very busy; he was travelling a lot, he had lost his phone, which couldn't be true as she only phoned him at his office and the most terrifying thought, *he didn't love her anymore.*

When she was at her most vulnerable, in the wee small hours, Mary let the doubts in.

Like why had Raoul never taken her to any of the posh restaurants he frequented, was he ashamed of her? Why has he never introduced her to his friends? Why had she never been invited to meet him at his office in the London Lafette building and why had he never taken her to his other home?

That's when Mary cried herself to sleep nearly every night; Mrs Grant was worried about her. As the weeks went past, Mary found she was losing heart, maybe he'd found someone from his own society, someone he could be proud of, someone more to his liking who wouldn't hold him back.

Grimacing at that idea, who was she kidding, hold him back from what? His name was already known throughout the world, he was a man of his word, his business ethics never questioned.

But this wasn't about business, was it; it was about a commitment he had made to her but had reneged on at the first opportunity.

Thankfully February was busy with preparations for St Valentine's Day celebrations. It helped Mary with the animosity she was starting to feel towards Raoul.

It was now the middle of March, and Mary received a surprise phone call from Raoul to say he would visit her the following afternoon when she finished work.

No questions on how she was, how did she spend Christmas, more importantly... did she miss him?

As it was the start of the week-end, Mrs Grant had left in the morning to catch the early train from Liverpool Street Station, to go down to Norfolk to stay for a week, Mary notified the estate manager to pick her up from the station.

Dressing warmly against the bitter cold, Mary wore her new black fitted trousers, and the new emerald green shirt and thick duffle coat she had been given for Christmas from Mrs Grant.

Pleased with the new helper Lily, as she was taking over more of Mrs Grant's work, making Sandy toe the line and pull her weight, she also filled in for Mary which left her more time for her arrangements.

Also today it would give Mary extra free time so she could have an undisturbed visit with Raoul.

# Chapter 18

Except it was late when he showed up and he never kissed her hello or embraced her, he appeared quiet, withdrawn and tense as though he had something on his mind, just like she did.

Oh yes did she ever.

He looked as though he had just stepped out of a fashion show. His ensemble was perfection; the pristine white shirt showed his tan and the superb cut of his bespoke suit plus the hand-made Italian leather shoes spoke of style and big money.

She caught a whiff of his expensive cologne that he had specially blended for him by a perfumery in Paris.

He insisted they go out for dinner although Mary had been hoping … well hoping for time alone with him.

He selected a small Italian restaurant in Mayfair where he was obviously well known; it had a rich wood dining room, with an extra-large mirror behind the bar. There were small individual private curtained areas, which the maître d' led them to.

The other diners stopped to look at them, but it was the women who gave him thirsty looks, like they wanted him to be their evening meal, what alarmed her most was he returned those looks.

What the hell was he doing?

Mary gave him a startled look, was she jealousy because he looked at other women, because he had never done that before in her company, so what happened to change him?

She should be used to them by now, but she knew she wasn't, she knew never in a thousand years would she be in their class but that was no excuse for him to ogle other women in her presence.

Being seated by the waiter as though she was someone important caused Mary to blush especially after he shook out the serviette and placed it on her lap. Presenting them with a menu, he said the wine waiter will come shortly and take their order.

Through all this Raoul was very quiet, almost cold in his attitude, it unsettled Mary, many times she tried to catch his eye but he wouldn't look at her.

"What would you like to start with? I will have the prosciutto-wrapped grissini breadsticks with cheese sauce, then shrimp scampi with pasta" When Mary didn't answer he raised his eyes from the menu.

"Mary?" His voice lacking warmth sent a shiver down her spine.

"What's wrong Raoul, why won't you look at me?"

The look he nearly gave her was frosty to say the least, but it landed somewhere over her right shoulder. Okay that made her more determined to find out what was wrong.

When she wasn't looking, he could see the worry in her beautiful lying eyes. Raoul snapped as the waiter returned "Please leave us, I will order later"

"Whoa Raoul, there's no need to snap at the poor man, what's got into you?" Mary's Black Dog of darkness raised its ugly head again and her doubts came back a thousand fold.

"Did I hear you right; are *you* of all people picking me up on my manners?" Raoul shot out of his chair. Taken aback for a moment, Mary stood up to go to him but he moved away from the table, his carriage stiff.

"Did you have a rough flight Raoul is that why you're cranky? Mary reached out to touch him, but he jerked away from her. "As I travel in my private jet I do not have rough flights, and I have been in London for the past three days. Now as you have completely ruined any thought I had of enjoying my meal. I will escort you home, I've had enough of the twenty questions" Briskly moving to the curtain he pushed it aside. Mary scrambled to collect her bag and hurried after him.

Her thoughts in chaos 'He had been in London and not let her know?'

The valet had brought the car round by the time Mary, blushing furiously as the other diner's watched Raoul storm out of the restaurant without her, and head towards the car clearly still angry.

Okay she thought he is definitely in a bad mood, best to keep my mouth shut until he took her home.

He never said a word; the tension inside the car was thick enough to cut with a knife. Mary sat with her fingers tied in a knot in her lap. Glancing at him she saw his hands gripping the steering wheel, his knuckles white.

She tried to think back had said or done something to upset him, and then common sense prevailed.

How could she have when he had not been in touch with her? Then she remembered what he said about being home for a few days. Turning her head she looked at the stern set of his jaw.

"Raoul, if you were home why didn't you get in touch with me?" He interrupted her.

"I said leave it, and stop whining, I cannot stand women who whine" Well she wasn't being spoken to like she was a bad-tempered child.

"No I won't leave it, what's got up your nose. You have been away for weeks and return in a shitty mood and then take it out on me. Well mate, I'm nobody's punching bag anymore, so say what bugging you?"

"What do you mean punching bag anymore?" His brow furrowing as he questioned her.

"Forget it; this is about your rotting attitude"

Then Mary saw they were at his hotel in Mayfair.

Right, so he wasn't taking her home or to his other place where ever that was, was he subtly telling her something? Maybe change of heart, but she knew something happened on this business trip, if it was a business trip?

Because before he went abroad, he had been full of love for her and miserable about missing her, then suddenly silence, especially when he went to America.

Driving to the front of the hotel, he leaped out of the vehicle, tossing the keys to the parking valet, and ignored the hand she held out to help her out of the car; he let the valet do it.

"You may have found your chauvinism, but you appear to have lost your good manners while you were away" Mary didn't care if she sounded bitchy, she'd had enough.

Totally ignoring her, he strode purposely past the beautiful receptionist, which was a first as he usually liked to talk to her; He stepped quickly towards the private lift, holding the door for her and tapping his foot impatiently waiting for her to catch up.

"Do you think you could move more swiftly, I do not have all day to wait for you?" Trying hard to ignoring his caustic words, Mary was sure the receptionist could hear everything he said as he hadn't modulated his voice, and she felt her heart sink.

All the way up to the penthouse, he ignored her as though she wasn't there.

Of course by this time Mary's gander was well and truly up. Nobody treated her like she didn't exist anymore. Been there, gone through that.

Entering the apartment Raoul went straight to the bar, poured himself a drink and swallowed it in one go, never asking if she wanted a drink, which went against his normal good manners. So Mary stood at the door waiting to be invited in, he turned to speak to her and said "For goodness sake why are you standing out there?" Shuffling her feet she raised a firm chin "Why I'm waiting to be invite in as I said earlier you appear to have misplaced your good manners"

Rolling his gorgeous eyes, he snapped "Please come in"

Mary thought he looked uncomfortable, like he didn't want to be here, but that was silly, this was his home … actually come to think of it, it wasn't his *proper* home, as he had stated he had a home somewhere else.

Ok, her head was going round in circles. Taking deep breathes; Mary moved towards him "Raoul, you didn't answer my question, why you never called me when you were home early. Did someone or something upset you in New York, is that why you needed time to yourself, is that why you are angry?"

His voice hardened as he looked at her "Yes I suppose you could say that. I needed time to sort through a problem by myself; plus I had a very disturbing meeting in New York. Then because I had promised you fidelity and I was desperate for sexual relief it was hard keeping the other women at a distance, but I knew you were here waiting for me"

Right, she really didn't need to hear about the other women or his constant boasting about his prowess with these women. She knew he attracted women like a magnet; Raoul continued, "You were here weren't you Mary?"

Walking towards her, he slide her coat from her shoulders to fall to the floor unheeded as his hand moved skilfully under her shirt and he felt her breast swell at his touch.

Leaning into her neck he pinched her earlobe between his sharp teeth, his barely there kiss not making contact with her lips, no matter how much she strained to catch his kiss. His breath fragrant with whiskey and his body scent was all around her, Mary's resistance melted at his touch, her temper gone., after all Mrs Grant had taught her how to forgive.

"You were here weren't you?" he persisted.

"Of course I was here, where else would I be, why keep asking me that. It was a busy time in the shop"

"But I phoned you at home last week-end and you never picked up, why?" Then Mary remembered she went down to Rainbow Gardens that week-end to help her friend.

Smiling at the memory, she was about to answer him when he changed tactics and said "I have missed you so much, it seems like eons since I last caressed you"

Mary found herself being carried off into the bedroom. Whoa, why the sudden change of behaviour? Was he using sex to avoid answering her questions?

She hated this room; it reminded her of the other woman he brought here, although he never admitted it, he always seemed to dodge that question as well. His caresses seemed to be different, more forceful, more intense like … ruthless. But he was caressing her and Mary couldn't help moaning, closing her eyes to saviour the love he was giving her.

Except it didn't feel like love, it felt … off.

"I need you; I cannot wait for our union, say you want this too?" When she didn't immediately answer his hands moved to her hips gripping them hard, and lifting her lower body into his very erect shaft.

It gave her a lot of pleasure to think she could move him to such a degree that he showed how much she meant to him even in his anger. Hope was alive in her heart again; he was still the man she desired.

Having promised herself she would wait until her wedding day before losing her virginity, Mary knew she could not wait either, they were getting married anyway, so would it make any difference, now or then? He was the man she loved and … yes, she would give him her virginity now.

"Raoul you know I am a virgin, please be gentle" Mary lifted her arms and he pulled her shirt off, then her bra, and was about to stroke her breasts when he spied the scars on her upper arms for the first time.

Reeling back in revolt in shock, he exclaimed "Good God what is this, what are these ugly marks on your arms?" Then he turned her round and saw worse scars on her back, the look of utter disgust on his face scared her.

"Mon Dui, who had done this to you?"

Mary felt a moment of panic then moved onto her back again "Forget them, this day is for us, please kiss me my love"

Seeing the indecision in his eyes, she tugged his head down but at the last moment he turned his head slightly and nibbled along her jawline then down her throat, to the tip of one protruding nipple.

Immediately that blocked all other thought as she gave herself up to the throbbing desire her body longed for.

"Later we will discuss this but I have to know are you alright with this Mary? I do not want you to do anything against your will, but I will make it like heaven for you, I am an expert at pleasing the female body, but you already know all about heaven don't you?"

There he goes again, boasting about his other conquests. Sometimes it was hard for her to understand his behaviour, like now, one minute he is solicitous and caring, the next swaggering about his successes.

Trying to hide her annoyance with a watery smile "What's with all the talk of your past conquests Raoul, you don't have to remind me how cocky you are, I see it on the social pages and in magazines. At least I hope they are in the past Raoul, you wouldn't lie to me about something as important as that would you?"

# Chapter 19

The look he gave her should have told her a different story, but she was too far gone to pay heed to it as his hands on her were making magic, clouding her mind to the point she forgot what the question was.

He was touching her everywhere except on her arms, but she didn't care, she was passed that, this was her time to become a woman.

She loved and trusted this man unconditionally.

Observing him as he unzipped his trousers, Mary is shocked at the size of his manhood, her equilibrium knocked for a six, he was bloody huge.

At least she thought he was, because she had no reference to go by never having seen a naked man, but from the embarrassing book she had read, he looked bigger than the pictures.

Would it hurt when he made love to her, well, she wasn't a coward, and would just grit her teeth because no way was she stopping now.

She was determined to become a woman at last, excitement was rippling through her body, she knew not what for, but she wanted what was to come.

His voice was impatient when he answered her "Are you assuming I have had relationships with these women, I would have to be superman to keep up with them all. Not that I would find it difficult to satisfy them, as I have been told I have great stamina, but I prefer quality to quantity, as you appear to go for quantity"

Gob smacked at this, Mary retaliated, "There you go again making assumptions about me Raoul, and I'm getting a bit peeved. No, I have never been taken to heaven, I told you I am a virgin, and I have never allowed a man close to me emotionally or sexually, only you"

The look of disbelief that flashed across his face disconcerted her for a moment. No, it had to have been something else; Raoul was just impatient for her that's all, he had given his word to her he had been celibate.

"For someone who recons he's been celibate for a long time you talk too much, how about some action?" she said, then trailed a finger from his throat to his delicious lips that she hadn't kissed yet.

His breath stopped immediately then gained momentum as he lowered his head his lips slowly suckled again on a rosy pink nipple while his fingers manipulated the peak of the other.

"Please Raoul kiss me?" Mary's heavy breath making her voice hoarse with longing, her fingers rifling through his silky hair, her breathing becoming rapid the closer his hand got to her sex. His touch was very rough as he inserted one finger to ascertain how wet she was, if she was ready for him.

Squirming at the unusual object in her

body Mary voiced her objection, "Ouch, stop Raoul that hurts" But all she heard was his breathing accelerate as he wrapped a hand round her bottom as he pulled her closer.

He fitted his body into the cradle she made by opening her legs, she could feel his engorged penis touched the lips of her sex, and suddenly he powerfully pushed inside her.

His moan was loud and long, hers was agonised.

No, she didn't like this at all; it felt like an invasion of her body, his forceful action rough, so Mary tried to pull away from him, wanting to eject it, pushing at his chest to no avail. "Raoul, please stop, it's uncomfortable"

Only he wasn't listening, but he was watching her "Sorry, I'll be more careful, just relax Mary, you will enjoy it"

Closing her eyes for a moment, she realised she wasn't enjoying it, there was no finesse in the coupling, no talk of love, no tenderness, just his rapid movement as he nearly pulled completely out of her then slamming back into her again; no there was certainly nothing gentle about his actions.

Mary opened her eyes and saw he was still watching her, which frightened her because there was no warmth, only icy coldness staring back at her.

What was going on? Was this his love for her? Surely not, she had read in books love was glorious, a matching of souls, a commitment to each other, a joining of hearts, and why hadn't he kissed her properly, come to think of it he hadn't kissed her at all; also he was still fully clothed.

Was she wrong to expect softness, gentleness, loving words, all of the things she felt for him, but she received none of that. It all felt cold, mechanical, like a duty to be performed.

Like vengeance.

Suddenly Raoul's body went into overdrive, his movements quickening, along with his breathing, and then he moaned as his warm seed shot into her before he went unbelievably stiff collapsing onto her.

Mary was confused, what had just happened?

Raoul instantly rolled off her, sitting on the edge of the mattress, his rapid breathing of a moment ago becoming steadier, and then he drew in deep breath. Then he zipped his pants and straightened his clothes.

Mary leaned up on her elbows unable to believe her eyes, watching him for a moment.

"Raoul, was that it, are you angry with me was I supposed to feel something other than being used?"

Then she got annoyed when he walked away from her. "Will you please answer me, what just happened?" Again he ignored her and walked towards the bedroom door.

Jumping off the bed she started searching for her clothes. She was in such a dither she put her shirt on inside out, her knickers were useless, so she went commando and then she couldn't find her bra, shrugging she pulled on her trousers.

Whirling round, she looked at him, her green eyes spitting fire "Raoul, what the hell was that. Did you just slack your sexual thirst on me, and why have you not kissed me? What's going on, one minute you're very caring, making sure I'm comfortable and then next you're freezing me out. No more fobbing me off, I want to know why? If something upset you when you were away, you need to tell me so I can help you. Furthermore why didn't you contact me when you come home early, Raoul I want answers now, something's not right, please tell what is it?"

Bending her head, she tried to gather her crazy thought, maybe he found someone else, and he was finished with her.

Puzzlement shone in her eyes when she raised her head, then turned to anger at his look of revulsion as she asked "Why did you not undress Raoul to make love to me, or is that the norm with you?

Turning away from her, Raoul sauntered into the lounge his back stiff as a rod as he moved to the bar, picking out the same whiskey bottle he had before pouring a good measure into a crystal glass. Mary hurried after him.

"I asked you a question"

"No you did not, you demanded, I do not

answer to demands" His voice cold enough to cause freeze burns.

'Stop procrastinating, what's going on? Did you just use me for sex?"

Mary looked at Raoul, his nonchalant stance was deceptive, and she could see he was holding on to his temper, ready to explode. Well so was she more than ready, whatever had upset him he had no right to push his bad mood on her.

The hands thrust into his trouser pockets only emphasized his clenched fists; his cheeks slightly flushed, his eyes cold.

His laughter was beyond belief, it was harsh and nasty. "Use *you* for sexual relief; you have to be joking …"

Mary let him have it with both barrels "Okay out with it, I know you're bursting to lay it on me so go ahead, I will let you have your say, and then I'll have mine"

Raoul threw her a filthy look.

Mary blinked the haze from her eyes, my God, where was all this hostility coming from, and why was it aimed at her?

Tensing at the angry tone in his voice, Mary lowered her head then and took a step back, balking at what she needed to get off her chest, the suspicions, *which he had perpetuated,* the doubts she had tried so hard to ignore.

Knowing she would have no peace of mind until she talked to him of what their relationship had turned into by his actions. A disaster … and her heart shattered.

"Right, time for you to answer some hard questions, I'm confused by your behaviour since your trip to New York. You phone me when you arrived; sounding pretty amiable, then suddenly, nothing for weeks, you changed Raoul, you have been home for three days and don't tell me. Then you start treating me like something rotten under your hand-made leather shoes, the way you hurt me when you thrust into my body. Did I do something wrong before you went away; you have to help me here because I've never been in a situation like this before?"

His look surveyed her from head to toe before walking towards the widows.

"And you think I have? What are you accusing me of Mary, please be more specific, you know I am no good at reading your confused mind?" Contempt was rich in the accusation he threw over his shoulder.

"I refuse to stand here and let you belittle me, if you have a guilty conscience about something, then have the goodness not to take it out on me" Sweeping her long hair away from her flushed face, Mary tried desperately to control the quiver in her voice.

Her doubts were starting to override her common sense.

"All I'm getting is empty speechmaking from you" Mary interrupted him "Raoul, you have gone completely cold on me, you had sex with me, you didn't make love with me, you have not kissed me either, why?"

"And I have to say, it was very unsatisfactory, you need more practice, or have you had too much sex and do not care anymore"

"Say one more horrible thing about me again and you'll be sorry, have you met someone else, are you having an affair, is that it, is it the red headed woman you always have hanging on you, are you breaking up with me?"

"Mary you have a perchance to create a situation that does not exist, at least with me you do. Keep your wild imagination to yourself. You know Leslie is a valued colleague to me, but you want to make it into something dirty, I won't allow you to malign her"

Well, you could have knocked her over with a feather, who was talking about Leslie? Certainly not her, right he brought the woman into the conversation, so she now wanted the truth.

Wait a minute, Leslie who?

Clenching her hands Mary was ready for a fight; she didn't survive on the worst streets of London without learning to fight.

"Who the hell is this Leslie, is that the person you call Les when you're on the phone? Is Les a woman but you make out she's a man to me? Is she the person I saw you with the day you had me make a flower arrangement in this very apartment. Is she your very special lady friend you told the hotel manager about? Is she the pregnant lady I saw you with at the hospital the day you cancelled our date because, quote 'you had to go away again for an important meeting' I know she wasn't the woman you saw in Singapore giving her a diamond necklace and then kissing her. Is she another one of your women you promised me you were not involved with, you're a bloody liar Raoul Lafette"

He was stunned, how did she know he was with Leslie at the hospital the day he cancelled their meeting, then he remembered seeing her across the road.

"That's enough, do not talk about that precious lady, she puts your attempt to act like a woman to shame, and Camille was my mistress, and a great lover which you will never be"

Mary reeled back as if he had smacked her.

Blanching at his cruel words Mary shoulders went straight back "How dare you, are they the reason you're in a stinking mood, what did your lovers do, drop you because you couldn't satisfy them, like you couldn't do it for me?"

Oh no, she should shut up; she's not an

aggressive person, but she was fighting for her reputation.

Mary saw his face shut down and knew she had hit a nerve somewhere "Is she the reason you didn't come and see me when you returned to London, is she the reason you don't hold or kiss me anymore? I know we have only been together for a few months, but *you* opened up this relationship, *you* are the one who pursued me relentlessly, *you* are the one who declared your love for me before I even knew what love was between a man and woman. Now you spring the cold treatment on me. Tell me, do your feelings for your so called *colleague* take precedence over your feelings for me Raoul, or have you crossed the line and made your friend your lover?"

# Chapter 20

Closing her eyes at the way she had phrased her defence Mary did not like it, why had she let him get the better of her, Mrs Grant would be ashamed of her.

Please God give me strength, because she knew without a doubt he no longer wanted her or her love.

Praying his answer would be in the negative to all her questions, Mary was on the point of collapse when she saw the fury in his eyes, and knew she had ruined any future she wished for with this man.

Raoul froze at the accusations Mary was firing at him; he could feel his temper explode.

"Who do you think you're talking to? You're a piece of work do you know that. You're also a lying bitch, you volunteered the information you were a virgin when I told you I had grown tired of the women who only wanted me for my money. But you cheated and lied to me. Feelings for you, don't make me laugh, to have feelings a person would have to care, which I certainly do not"

"What, you just wait right there, no one calls me a liar or a cheat. You called me a bitch, get your bloody facts right, the only bitch in this conversation is you, and the only cheat here is you, the only liar here is you. You have been seeing the woman Leslie behind my back; in fact you led me to believe Leslie was a man. Also you told me you were single when I asked if you were in a relationship, then I see a photo of you with another woman in Singapore and you're all over each other like a rash. What have I done to deserve your hate? I swear I have never lied to you …"

Raoul shouted her down "Yes you did and you're still lying" His temper completely out of control. "I wish with all my being, with all that is me that I had never got involved with a sleazy piece of trash like you"

Her heart sinking Mary took a steading breathe "If you had wanted to break-up with me you didn't have to go to these extreme lengths"

"It makes my skin crawl to think I let you touch me, I trusted you, you miserable excuse for a woman" Again Raoul was shouting, this time right in her face, that was the last straw. Mary pushed at his rock hard chest, and he raised his hand to strike her, she immediately lifted her fists to her face in a protective gesture.

Her actions brought Raoul to his senses. Mon Dieu, he had nearly hit a woman. "See what you have brought me to; I have never in my life raised a hand to anyone, least of all to a woman"

"I have not brought you to this action, you have done that yourself with your secrets and lies, saying one thing and doing the opposite, answer me, what have I done to deserve all this hate? As I said we have only been in a relationship for a short while, and you were the one to insist we wouldn't have sex until our marriage" Mary's voice was shaky as she asked these questions, but she held her ground.

"I will tell you what you did, I saw you in America, at that night club, with *two* men, doing dirty dancing with one man, being provocative and sexual in your movements, my God you were practically having sex on the floor while all the other dancers watched. Then you left with the *two* men kissing them, and saying you wanted the middle of the bed that night. You did not see me in the shadows when you left; you were too engrossed in the men. You disgust me you cheating whore"

Staggering back from his angry person Mary intruded into his nasty words "You're a raving lunatic, I have never had a lover, man or woman, I have never been to America, I told you I have never travelled outside of England …"

"There you go again lying you're head off. If you were a virgin, why was there no blood on the sheets, why did you feel no pain when I penetrated you? If it was not me who breached you're hymen Mary who was it, was it the two men you were very close to in America or do you open your legs for any man in trousers?"

His cruel words hit Mary like bullets from a machine gun, tearing into her body ... killing her heart.

Killing her love

"Get out of my sight, I do not want to see you anymore, the sooner I am rid of you the cleaner I will feel. For your information the woman I marry in the future, I will love with all my heart and I will be proud of her and respect her when she has my babies, she will have my protection and undying love, but she will never be a cheating whore like you, now get out"

Raoul turned his head but he was not quick enough. He watched her beautiful body tremble. Then he made a big mistake and looked in her eyes that used to shine with laughter, but no more. All he saw was devastation and heartbreak then he watched the life leave her body.

Never in his life had he seen another

human being literally die before his eyes, but he saw it in Mary's.

He saw her love for him die that day.

As Mary backed away from his cruel words, she could feel the edge of darkness pulling her painfully. The darkness had never been a friend to Mary; she had fought it with all her being, and won. She would not let that Black Dog drag her down into the gutter again.

Mary lifted her chin; she was stronger now than she had ever been, thanks to Mrs Grant, she now knew what love was. Not the physical act, but the emotion that she had once felt coursing through her body for this man. Yes, she could now put a name to the joyous passion she could feel as it was wrenched out of her heart by his cruel words.

She scooped her handbag from the atrocious coffee table, pausing for a moment before stumbling to the door, then she straightened her shoulders, her head held high as she nearly closed the door behind her … then paused. She wasn't a quitter, so why start now.

Gathering her inner strength she threw the door open again, he watched her approach as she walked right into his personal space, he drew a harsh breath, he could still smell her fragrance, that was purely Mary.

"I have stood the barrage of innuendoes and insults you have thrown at me ..." He tried to interrupt her "No, you just shut up you arrogant prick and listen to somebody else's voice instead of your own for a change. Not everyone was born into luxury like you and your brother. Not everyone had a mother, never mind a mother *and* a father. You might not have been spoiled, but you were *loved* by somebody even if it was only your brother. You also had the security of status and money to help you in emergency situations, plus you had the warmth and protection of that brother's love, never fearing for your life or, who would attack you in the dark as you tried to sleep in any kind of shelter out of the freezing cold, even under a park bench hoping no one would see you, especially the park keeper who would lock you out, or sometimes wrapped in plastic to keep dry because you didn't have enough clothes to wear.

Do you even know what it's like *not* to be loved, *not* to have anyone, no matter who, to care for you. To wondered where your next bit of food is coming from. Have you ever raided garbage bins for any sort of food, for clothes of any kind so you don't freeze in winter?

I never knew my parents, I was raised by social services in foster homes and used and abused in them, hence my scars, I was used as an ashtray, and whipped with a cane until I bled when I was seven years old, so I ran away. Yes I also lived in the gutter for a year, then when I was eight years old Mrs Grant found me, and gave me the only protection I ever knew in my life, also the warmth and comfort of her love"

Swiping at the tears in frustration Mary continued "I vowed to make my future better, to learn from my mistakes and to drag myself out of the gutter, but always to be true to myself. With Mrs Grant's help I did just that"

Mary didn't want to go back into

her putrid past, to let loose that bloody darkness, the cause of all her misery, but she had beat it, she had made the blackness her friend. She had fought all her life to be a better person, so no way was she letting this spoiled despot slander her name with his prejudices.

The pain of her past and his accusations was reflected in her voice as she faced him "I can't change my past but by God I can and will change my future. Not you or any other small minded bigot is going to stop me, so you can take you're allegations and shove them where the sun don't shine, You said you have never had a virgin, how do you know about breaking the hymen, about blood?"

Moving to the door Mary paused for a minute then looked back at him. "I don't understand why I'm not a virgin, I don't know anything about bleeding, or anything about sex, but I *do* know you're not as clean as you think you are, I feel sorry for you, you have blackness in your heart, and you have let it rule your life. I know what darkness is. Raoul, black is not the new fun colour if you use it for misery. Black is a colour to respect, no matter if it's fabric or skin. Never let it become an emotion, only you can change it, to make it a happy colour, to make it your friend.

Hear me well, for the untruths and filthy words you have called me today I will make you beg for my forgiveness. You could have easily checked with the passport office that I have never held a passport, but that would have given you no reason to break your promise to me. No matter what the motivation or excuse you may have in the future to contact me, I vow by all I hold precious you will suffer for the mistakes you have made against me today"

Raoul watched her leave just as his phone rang, but she had not closed the door properly on her departure, as he could hear her sobbing, plus she would have heard him answer his phone, and call the person 'his love' and enquire about their baby boy"

Looking at the door Mary had left by, he knew he was being a total swine, hoping she had heard him talking to Leslie, but he did not have to rub her nose in it did he?

Then he moved to the drinks cabinet and poured a very large whiskey then threw it back, not even tasting it as the liquid burned his throat.

Turning suddenly, he threw the full bottle at the pristine wall, but he still felt a bastard. Standing by the large window he watched early morning lighten the sky, and he could also see his reflection, and did not like the man looking back at him, he called himself all sorts of a coward.

Plus she was right; he had blackness in him to have hurt her the way he did. God in heaven what had he done, he had never acted like that in his life. He'd had his head stuck up his ass, and was not thinking straight.

He had sprouted innuendoes without proof at the woman he thought he loved, and she was right he could have, should have made a point of making enquiries about what he saw, instead of taking it for granted.

Alright, so he had seen her, or thought it was her, with two other men … no he could not get past that especially the way she had danced with one man. The other dancers had stood and applauded them.

It had been disgusting to watch.

Since when had he turned into a prude? Hadn't he enjoyed the pleasure of twins at the same time, Mary was right, he is a hypocrite.

Maybe he was not that much different from his elder brother after all, maybe he liked kinky sex.

Of course he had to take into account what she said; it could easily have been checked. He should have got Ramsey Investigations onto it immediately.

Not known how long he stood looking out of the window, except it was now very bright, trying to close his mind to the devastation he saw in Mary's eyes, he turned and moved wearily to his bedroom,

Raoul surveyed the unmade bed, visualising what had transpired earlier and felt shame. He sat wearily on the bed then lifted the sheet to his nose; yes her perfume was still present.

Never in his life had he deliberately used a female for sex, he had never left a partner wanting; his creed had always been to satisfy even the most hardened woman, before taking his own pleasure, and with pride he had never failed in that activity.

Until now she never reached an orgasm; she also said he had hurt her. Clutching his head between shaking hands he felt disgust and humiliation that he had only sought satisfaction for himself. At least he proved a point; she had not been a virgin, and that was irrefutable, no way could she get out of that.

———— ❀ ————

Sitting on the bed he let his mind drift back to the incident in New York that started all this mayhem.

No way was he going to lose out on this deal to that bastard who has been chasing the same contract. He had worked to long and too hard and he would bring it to its conclusion. All he needed was an hour to regroup his thoughts.

New York was bristling with holiday makers and he loved the hype of the different cultures. Arriving at his hotel, one of his newer purchases, he viewed the foyer with a critical eye, happy at the excellent attention of the staff to the customers. He had made no one aware of his arrival, but the manager was on hand to welcome him.

After his luggage was delivered to the penthouse and rapidly unpacked by a maid, he made a call to his sweet Mary, unfortunately it went unanswered. She had said she was staying at home to catch up with some reading, maybe he'll try again later.

As he headed for his study, he heard his private lift stop, turning round he saw his beautiful blonde personal assistant emerge. Smiling at her as she checked the tablet in her hand, she brought up the pertinent information he had requested.

# Chapter 21

Smiling, she said "Hello Raoul, you will be pleased to learn the other party challenging the deal has pulled out of the contract. It appears they were a rogue company trying to up the price of your bids. Your legal boys jumped on them immediately and they withdrew quick smart. We think they had a fake office on Lexington Avenue, near some club called "LQ", I won't know the exact address until the investigators get back to me"

This very good news, Raoul thanked her and told her to inform the rest of the team and herself to finish and relax for the next two days before returning to London.

Later that same evening Raoul found himself at a loose end so he decided to pay a visit to the fake office just to satisfy his curiosity.

Finding the bogus address he was not surprised the legal boys done intensive investigations on the rogue client. Then wandering down the street he found himself near the club his PA mentioned. He was not enamoured to Latin music, so why he here?

Standing outside the club he read the name The LQ, meaning The Latin Quarter, pushing the door open, he ventured inside, to the sound of fast Spanish music. Seeing he was here he might as well have a look.

The foyer was designed in typical Spanish style. A curtain separated the room and he stepped aside to allow a couple to leave then entered the room where people were dancing … and received the biggest shock of his life.

His Mary was dancing with another man, no, not dancing; they were seducing each other with their body movements. She was all dressed up and wearing make-up, she looked beautiful … and she was in the arms of another man.

Shaking his head to try and clear it of the sight of his girlfriend in a sexual dance. She was running her hands down his body, and allowing him the same freedom.

In a rage Raoul was ready to tear the stranger to bits, then the dance suddenly finished, and Mary leaned into the man and kissed him on both cheeks, they were sweating profusely and laughing, her green eyes dark with emotion.

God he loved her husky laugh.

They were joined by another man and he could not believe his ears when he overheard her saying 'I bag the middle of the bed tonight you losers' The threesome did not see him in the shadow of the curtain as they passed by. Grabbing a taxi he followed them to their hotel.

Full of white hot anger, he stayed outside their hotel all night and saw them all leave early the following morning; Mary gave them both a kiss as she got into a different vehicle.

Exhausted, he hailed a taxi to his hotel.

Looking at his reflection he saw bitterness in his dark eyes, his face drawn and dark with bristled, needing a shave, his cloths dishevelled.

After a shower he alerted his pilot to get ready to return to London. Sitting on the end of the bed, his hands shaking, unable to believe what he had seen. Reaching forward he phoned housekeeping to send a maid to pack his bags.

How could his sweet Mary behave like a slut, like a prostitute? She was always nervous around men, always felt uneasy in their company.

Ha, not any more by the way she was flouncing around the strangers. He believed her love was only for him and he had taken her at her word, what an idiot. Mon Dieu, he felt betrayed, again, she also made him feel … unclean.

--- ✳ ---

After a heavy working flight to London, he had every department in his vast network put a block on any and all calls from Mary

Smith, but no matter what he tried Raoul could not get the picture of his gentle Mary behaving like a slut out of his head, but he was more than ready to confront her.

Then the enormity of what his confrontation would do to their relationship struck him hard, so he decided to calm down, no point in going off half-cocked when he was so angry. His brother had warned him once about never being able to take back angry words spoken in temper.

So he cooled his heels for a few days by working flat out before contacting her, he would take her out for an evening meal then confront her. Maybe it would be more convenient to wait until she finished work late in the evening.

Yes he would have the private conversation in his apartment, less of an embarrassment if she got angry.

Too late, he had lost his temper, something he rarely did, how could she say it was not her when he saw her? He could have reached out and touched her. Oh yes, it definitely was her.

As for her saying she had never left England well Ramsey Investigators will put an end that nonsense, they would get the answers he wanted, her lies would be easy to check, she would have known he could easily check her alibi or didn't she care?

Never in his life had he used such language to a female, he always treated them with good manners, with gentleness.

He needed a break, needed to get right away from London. He would return to Singapore and forget this woman. As of this moment she is dead to him, so he would celebrated his freedom by working hard and playing even harder.

Raoul was not choosy about the women he associated with anymore, he only required they were slim, tall, had short hair and did not have green eyes.

In the following six months Raoul was determined to reach the name of billionaire extraordinaire. He pulled off exceptional business deals, attaining his goals, but his reputation as a playboy became known far and wide.

Travelling so much became a panacea for him, but not to his team as they were finding it difficult to keep up with him. His personal assistant tried to keep the peace but even she was losing sleep over his irregular tight schedules.

In the six months after his break-up with Mary, he lost himself in hard work to the detriment of his staff, who complained to his personal assistant about the long hours he had them working, he called a meeting. This was his business and he would run it his way.

"Right, what is this nonsense about work hours; you all get extra bonuses for the hours, right. Here is an alternative, you work my hours or you all find employment elsewhere … without a reference"

He walked out and let them discuss their problem.

No one left his place of work.

Right, no more was he going to be taken for a ride by anyone. So everybody knuckled down and business resumed. Although

Raoul did alternate his staff to give them some sort of life. Just because his life had gone down the toilet did not mean theirs had to as well.

He wanted staff to be happy, even if he could not. Mon Dieu, enough of this self-pity.

Back in Singapore he was going to paint the town *rouge*.

Raoul kept his word; he had beautiful women vying for his attention and he did not disappoint them, but he felt nothing, maybe his libido had gone on a permanent holiday because he felt no stirring in his body for any of these luscious women.

He took two of the most beautiful women he had been interested in before he met Mary, and they went to Marina Bay Sands; He swam in the rooftop infinity pool with them, he made them feel special with his personal attention, and they went all out to make him feel, both of them touching him sexually, trying to arouse him … but nothing.

He took them on the Gondola ride, and to the exclusive shops like Gucci, Versace,

Prada, buying clothes, shoes, bags, for them but he refused their pleas for jewellery when they deliberately stopped at Tiffany.

He escorted them to their suite and they again tried to excite him ... to no avail, he went home alone.

Frustrated!!!

Next day they visited Gardens by the Bay, and strolled through the world's largest greenhouse the Flower Dome, then through the Cloud Forest as the ladies wished to see the magnificent waterfall.

Later he watched as they shared their delight at the Garden Rhapsody, and the beautiful light display.

Then he went home to his apartment in Scott's Rd ... alone.

And all it did was fill him with ... loneliness.

Months later Raoul was going crazy with the situation, as no amount of self-seeking, over-indulged females could awaken his body or bring his dead heart to life. Under no circumstances could he tolerate this situation.

After a while to his embarrassment, the other women had gone around his friends in Singapore and complained about his failure to connect with them, so they tried to cheer him up by introducing him to the most beautiful, well known woman in Singapore who was famous for her sexual prowess

She was now sitting opposite him at Orchard Rd's revolving restaurant 'The top of the M' having an intimate dinner for two, and still he felt nothing, his conversation was spasmodic at best, he could not rid himself of the shame he felt in his heart.

His appetite, his emotions, and his sex drive had all evaporated, but his manners were impeccable, no matter what Mary said about them, as he bade the beauty good night at her apartment.

To say she was disappointed was mild, she was furious, and told him never to expect her company in the future.

And he could not give a damn, he wanted his life back, he wanted to feel alive once more, and by God he decided to get to the bottom of the riddle that was … Mary.

Standing outside the door of Raoul's penthouse, Mary tried so hard to hold back the heart breaking sobs, but it was so difficult. He hadn't even cracked a sweat when he was shouting her down. My God, the scorn and hate in his voice cut her to pieces.

Where had her loving friend gone, where was the man who had continued to bombard her with tenderness and care, who made it known he was hers and she was his, that they were a couple in a serious relationship.

Where had that man gone? How she needed a friend at this ugly time in her life, except she didn't have the one friend she wanted because he had thrown her love and friendship back in her face.

Mary sobbed, not realising their relationship had a used by date.

She would go home to her friend, the only woman who had shown her love, who has never let her down, and would stand by her no matter what because that's what friends did, and Mary desperately needed to discuss the present situation with her before she lost all sense of sanity.

Her mind keep returning to what Raoul had said, jeez, she had never been out of London, except to go down to Norfolk; It must be because he wanted to end their relationship that he has cooked up this ridicules story.

Mary knew all along he had strong feelings for a woman, even before they had become an item themselves. Also, hadn't he requested she made a loving floral display for him on his instructions for *'A very special woman'*, and hadn't she seen that same woman in his arms, all over him like climbing ivy, and he was doing likewise, with his arms holding her tightly to his muscular body? A body that had been wrapped round her own not more than an hour before.

Shaking her head to clear the hideous last few hours, Mary found it difficult to hide the fact she was upset when she caught the tube home to Islington.

No matter how often she wiped her eyes, the tears still came. One lady sitting opposite gave her a scornful look, eyeing her inside out shirt, because Mary had forgotten to put on her jacket, while a little old lady next to her gave her handful of tissues and patted her back as she left the tube.

The kindness of the old woman hit Mary's heart and strengthened her resolve to rise from the dirt Raoul had thrown at her; it also helped to stem the flow of tears.

Stuffing the tissues into the pocket of her trousers, she walked the short distance to her flat, only just starting to feel the cold; also she was feeling very self-conscious with no knickers on. Thank goodness it wasn't raining, but the wind had an icy bite to it.

Hugging her arms to keep warm, Mary checked her watch; she really wanted to talk to Mrs Grant, but first she desperately needed a shower, to try and wash the shame Raoul had covered her with from her stressful body.

# Chapter 22

Turning the corner, Mary was puzzled to see a police car outside the shop. Closing her eyes for a fraction, she drew in a deep breathe, okay so it looked like her bad day wasn't over yet.

Oh God what now, hasn't she had enough to cope with today, her first thought was 'Don't tell me Raoul had set the police on her' but why would he?

Hurrying forward Mary addressed the officer "Good morning sir can I be of assistance, do you want to speak to the owner, unfortunately Mrs Grant is in Norfolk this week-end"

The police officer asked who she was

and asked to view her credentials, but Mary asked the officer to come inside the shop out of the cold wind.

Inside the shop he continued to ask what her relationship was to Mrs Grant. Satisfied by her answers, he explained they had been trying to contact a staff member who knew the patient, but it was early Sunday morning and of course the shop was closed. They were relieved when they saw Mary; then explained about Mrs Grant's accident, just outside the train station in Norfolk.

"No that can't be right she only left yesterday" The officer excused himself to answer the beeping item on his shoulder.

Returning to her he said that was the local constabulary notifying him the patient had died from her injuries.

Covering her eyes she asked "What about the driver, was he hurt?" Mary moaned in distress at the affirmative, the officer put a hand out to steady her as she stumbled; she clutched his arm like a vice, tears streaming down her face, shaking her head.

"No sir, there has to be some mistake,

if you hang on a minute I will contact my friend …?"

The officer checked some details on his phone then spoke softly seeing the distress etched on Mary's face "I am sorry, there has been no mistake Miss, can I get a friend or someone to come stay with you to help you?"

Stunned by the news, the fat tears flowing unchecked from tortured eyes as she answered "No sir, Mrs Grant was my only friend. I must contact her lawyer about what's to happen now to the shop and staff. Thank you sir for your tolerance, I'll be alright"

"Well if you're sure, I have written down the information you will need if you go to the authorities, again my felicitations for the loss of your friend"

The officer tipped his hand to his hat as he left her.

Before Mary could phone Mrs Grant's lawyer the following morning, he showed up on very early with a heavy set middle aged man and explained he was Mrs Grant's nephew Peter Dunk. The rotund man informed Mary he was selling the shop immediately.

Mary was astounded by this news, and was angry for the staff who were about to lose their job. Sandy wasn't too worried as she said she was going to leave anyway, but Lily and Mary were cross at not being given sufficient notice. He told Mary to vacate the flat by the end of the week, and he wanted the keys to the van.

She told him the van was hers, and showed him the registration papers, then told him to get his facts right as he needed to give her at least two weeks' notice.

How dare he tell her to leave her home, but without her friend, Mary didn't want to stay anyway, so she would move down to Rainbow Gardens and make that her permanent home.

But first she had to visit the funeral home as the nephew refused to pay for the funeral for his aunt, although the lady had already taken out funeral insurance, also a life insurance that the greedy nephew thought was his.

Well the lawyer soon put him right as

everything apart from the shop and any bills incurred during business was his problem, but everything else had been left to Mary.

Thank goodness the solicitor explained to Mary the property in Norfolk was hers, lock, stock, barrel, and that Mrs Grant had signed it over to Mary when she turned eighteen.

But that didn't stop the greedy man trying to get his hands on the property; unfortunately he hadn't reckoned, according to him, quote 'A country oaf of a lawyer that had the smarts to beat him' unquote.

Two days later when he was told it would cost him thousands of pounds to take his case to the high court, the case was dropped by him and the sign to sell the shop was put up in the window immediately.

The solicitor was very scathing when he informed Mary the man only wanted the money selling the shop would bring him, to feed his gambling addiction.

After the meeting in his office with Mary and Peter Dunk he read out the official will of Mrs Pamela Grant, letting the nephew know he had no claim on Rainbow Gardens and Mary Smith was the sole beneficiary to all properties, monies, vehicles.

Needless to say Mr Peter Dunk was not at all pleased with the outcome; he slammed out of the office with a crude exclamation.

Mary started informing the other businesses of Mrs Grant's demise, and cancelling pending orders she left the shop. Mary packed the van with a heavy heart saying goodbye to Lily, but offering her a place at Rainbow Gardens if needed, her offer was taken with alacrity.

Sandy had already left the previous day and Mary set off for Norfolk, not looking back at the establishment that had given her so much happiness; she would miss her little flat and garden.

Driving out of London Mary went over what the lawyer said, He explained that Mrs Grant knew her no good nephew might try and get his grubby hands on her late husband's house and land.

That's why she secured the house and all the land to Mary, also all the money Mr

Grant had left to his wife, which she had invested wisely over the years, also Mrs Grant's life insurance.

It was a substantial amount of money, enough for Mary not to have a worry financially in the future. Mary remembered sobbing in the solicitor's arms as he comforted her; she said "I miss her so much, to go on without her wisdom, her advice, and her kindness. She has been the only constant caring person in my whole life"

"That's why she left everything to you; she informed me of your love for the earth and of nature, which you would care for, also the people at Rainbow Gardens, was she wrong?"

The solicitor queried "No, she wasn't wrong, but I have a big job ahead of me as Rainbow Gardens needs to be brought into the present as it is sadly lacking for top professional advice that will also take it into the future. I will need time for the locals who use the Gardens to come to terms with my updating the equipment as such, but first I have to have time to mourn my friend, good afternoon sir"

Mary desperately needed time alone. How she wished Raoul was still with her and could give her support. She had been sick for a few days, and lost weight since she hadn't been eating properly, and with all the upheaval and Raoul's accusations it's no wonder her life was all out of kilter.

All she needed was time to heal, but when she returned home, there was unrest amongst the tenants who shared the gardens; understandably they were just as shocked at the passing of their friend.

As she had relayed to the lawyer, they were also very worried about their future in the Gardens. Mary tried to convince them once she found her footing as the new owner; she would explain her plans for the Rainbow Gardens hopefully to everyone's satisfaction.

Regrettably it took nearly two months and a tremendous amount of deliberation before they were all happy with the conditions Mary wanted to implement.

She thought they really had no option as the land now belonged to her. Mary was sorely tempted not to see the doctor, but she couldn't explain why she was so sick all the time. So here she was outside the surgery.

She was extremely apprehensive entering the examination room after updating in her medical details on the request form to the receptionist. The doctor was a long-time friend of Mrs Grant's; in fact she used to take Mary to Dr Fleming for her regular check-ups when she was a young girl.

On the doctors request the duty nurse asked Mary to remove her clothes then handed her a gown to put on, with the opening at the back.

Shivering more with nerves rather than the cold Mary glanced around the small drab examination room that the staff had tried to make cheerful with a few bright pot plants.

The nurse lifted the blood and urine specimens and said "I'll just take these to the lab, can you please hop up on the table and the doctor will be with you soon"

Heaving her tired body onto the cold examination table, she dangled her legs over the side, hoping the doctor wouldn't be long.

Quaking inside Mary tried to smile but it was a poor effort as the young girl had already left the room. Wishing she could stop shaking, Mary felt really worried.

Why was she so tired all the time, she was never under the weather this bad, even when she had the flu.

Well wasn't that was why she was here, to find out why was she so sick, and not coping with anything lately.

Mary was so deep in thought she had not heard the doctor come in and was standing right in front of her. Jumping at the doctor's sudden presence Mary exclaimed "Goodness Doctor Fleming, you move quietly" Laughing, she gently patted Mary's shoulder "No Mary, you were so deep in thought and not happy ones by the way you're clenching you're fists"

The local doctor of indistinguishable age began checking Mary's records. "Mary I'm so sorry about our friend, Mrs Grant is sadly missed already, she was a lady full of life, and expressed to me many times how much joy you gave her" At her softly spoken words Mary felt the ever present tears well up again.

Why couldn't she control her emotions lately, it has to be more than just missing her friend.

"I miss her every day, and her hilarious jokes, her quirky laugh, remember the time she told you about using her bulk weight to push a man out the door" At that memory of Raoul, Mary lift sad eyes to the doctor. "I miss her so much Doctor"

Nodding the doctor patted her on the shoulder then said "Give it time Mary, I'm told time will heal everything. Now back to you my girl, I know we spoke on the phone yesterday about you're sickness, that's why I requested you book an appointment with me as soon as possible. Is it just in the morning or does it last longer?" The doctor lifted Mary's hand to take her pulse, while watching her breathing then she took her blood pressure, frowning at the result.

Drawing a heavy breathe, Mary replied, "No, but sometimes it could last all day ..." Just then the desk phone rang, answering it the doctor replied in a soft voice "Please bring the results to me now"

"When did you have your last period Mary?"

"I have had very light ones up till now, why is that significant?" The nurse returned handing the doctor the recent report, which raised her eyebrows, then scribbled on the chart, giving the nurse some instructions, who quickly left the room.

Turning to Mary she said "Well my friend I'm happy to tell you that you're twelve weeks pregnant, I would like you to have an ultra sound while you're here Mary, its part of the procedure to ascertain if your baby is ok?" Mary is stunned,

How?

When … then she remembered, the protection must have failed, oh God no she was not ready for this startling news, and then a thought hit her. Could a person get pregnant when they didn't climax.

Mary nodded her permission to the doctor for the scan.

The technician rubbed a cold gel on Mary's stomach, the doctor grinned "Would you like to hear your baby's heartbeat my friend. I estimate your baby should be born between the twenty third and the twenty eighth of December by the look of this graph, hey you could have a Christmas baby, wouldn't that be lovely. Your own special Christmas present, are you pleased?"

Mary's smile said it all; the happiness on her glowing face was proof enough, then she cried, gently at first when she heard the baby's heartbeat, then huge gulping sobs racked her thin body. Doctor Fleming wrapped her arms around her patients shoulder, letting her cry it out.

"Do you want to talk about it Mary? Is this the first time you've cried since the funeral?" Mary's pain said it all.

"Oh Doctor Fleming, such a lot of bad things have happened to me lately, but what you have just told me gives me new hope, a life to look forward to now. A baby doctor Fleming, a baby I can call my family, who will love *me* for just being *me*"

"Of course your baby will love you, now isn't that something special to look to the future for. I will give you a copy of the scan, now I did notice your blood pressure was high so we will have to keep an eye on it, but you will have regular anti-natal clinics to attend and you know you can contact me anytime, for any reason, after all you're my friend"

To say Mary was speechless would be ludicrous, the doctor watched tears sliding down Mary's beautiful face again but this time they were tears of joy.

Unfortunately the doctor had to have a few questions answered, a few awkward questions. "Mary, I'm sorry but I need to ask you some probing questions, knowing how much you dislike the male species, I have to ask were you raped?"

# Chapter 23

Seeing the shocked expression on her patients face answered that question.

"Good God no, I was in a relationship which Mrs Grant knew about, it lasted about six months then he broke it off, accusing me of infidelity, while he was seeing someone at the same time, I even heard him talk to the other woman and ask after his son, so I owe him nothing."

"I'm sorry I had to ask ..."

"Can I ask you something doctor?"

"Of course, I am here for you Mary, in whatever capacity you require of me, you're my friend"

Blushing furiously Mary asked "When

Raoul made love to me he said something about me not being a virgin, that there should have been blood on the sheets, and there was none, my question is why wasn't there any blood, and can a woman get pregnant if she hasn't … well, you know ahm, climaxed, I don't understand it?"

The doctor was silent for a moment then looked at Mary "First of all, it doesn't matter if the woman has a climax or not, Mary, it is if the man's sperm is inside you, and if you don't use some sort of protection during intercourse. Now did Mrs Grant ever tell you she went into the facts of your time in foster care, about what happened to you and why she had your closed records in the children's court unsealed?"

Shaking her head Mary replied with a questioning look. "No?"

"I know the details but they are not nice, but I think you should know so you can move forward with a clear conscious. Mary you did nothing wrong, all the fault was laid at the feet of your foster carers. They were a nasty pair and should never have been allowed to foster little children.

Mrs Grant gave all the information to her lawyer and to disclose it to you when you asked, but I can tell you here and now you did nothing wrong my friend, you were a child"

Mary's hands were shaking as she clasped them in her lap, her eyes swollen from crying.

'Then why wasn't I a virgin like Raoul said?"

"Well my friend you were sexually assaulted when you were five years old by the foster father, also for the scars he left you with, but they covered it up by using an unscrupulous medical student who owed them money at the time, who has since served a prison sentence for more than one wicked crime. Shame the foster father died before he could be prosecuted, but they jailed his wife for participating, and not reporting him for child abuse. Mary, please try not to dwell on this information, look to the future with your beautiful baby, when you're a bit further in your pregnancy we will be able to determine the sex, you would like that wouldn't you?"

The shock of hearing what had happened to her as a little girl was something that would take time to sink in. Only then would she discuss the ramifications with the lawyer. She wondered if that was why she disliked men. Anyway that was a mission for the future when she could handle it better, at the moment she had a baby to celebrate.

"My God, how could I be so lucky, I really don't know anything about my parents only that I was sent to various foster placements, sorry I'm rambling, I'm so excited, but I'm also scared, a baby doctor, I will need a lot of help as I know nothing of babies?"

The smile on her face was lovely to see, the doctor had been worried Mary would be so upset at hearing about her early childhood that the knowledge of her baby would be insignificant, but Mary had come through as the doctor hoped she would.

"No problem my friend, I will gladly be available to advise you, and maybe baby-sit if needed, yes? Now Mary down to basics, you will need to eat regularly as you have lost a lot of weight, and rest as much as possible, but also do a small amount of light exercise. I would like to see you frequently in this first trimester as that is the most crucial time in any pregnancy, also we need to keep an eye on your blood pressure, ok"

"I have made Rainbow Gardens my permanent home now doctor, I intend to make a business out of the gardens and plots of land. I have already discussed this with the other tenants. I have been given some superb advice on how to proceed in that direction, but first I will start in the house and make it a home for my child"

"Oh my God, just listen to me Doctor Fleming, my child, I going to be a mother" And the tears started again "Ah Doctor Fleming do you have some advice to help me stop the tears as I can't seem to turn them off?'

Laughing the medic said "It's just hormonal, it is like a safety valve and will stop soon, have a good day my friend" As Mary left the surgery her mind was buzzing with all the things she would do with her baby. Her eyes were shining and it had nothing to do with tears.

Mary knew what it was like to grow up without parents, and if her little baby could have the love of both a mother and father... wait; she was getting ahead of herself, both parents, which would mean informing Raoul.

Except Mary would need to get legal counselling before she moved in that direction, but one thing she was absolutely sure of she would not allow Raoul to take her baby. He could have access or visiting rights, but that's all. Unfortunately in the following weeks every time Mary tried to contact Raoul, she was told he wanted no dealing with her, at any time or for any reason and to stop calling.

———— ❂ ————

Every time Raoul had a date with a glamourous woman he would made sure the paparazzi were present, the media would do the rest by circulating the photos and Mary would see them and realise what she had screwed up.

After three months he tried not to think

about her, but it was hard, every time he heard a husky laugh, he'd spin around, only to realise it was not her.

Then common sense kicked in, how could it be when he was in Singapore and she was presumably still in London.

The next six months were hard because he could not believe how much he missed her, not just in his arms, but her husky laugh, her tender smile, her smell of rosemary, her shyness, the way she blushed and most of all in his empty heart.

The loneliness was excruciating.

Then a report landed on his desk from Ramsey's, but it wasn't happy news. Mrs Grant, the lady who owned the flower shop had been killed in an accident, on the day he threw Mary out of his life, and the shop was sold by her loser of a nephew.

Merde, she would be devastated, he knew how much she respected the old lady. Suddenly he wanted to go to her and console her, to make things better ... but he knew he could not; he had well and truly screwed that relationship.

The report specified a nephew inherited

the shop and he was a single man with a bad gambling addiction and regrettably it had ended his life to a gang boss he owed huge amounts of money to before the Ramsay investigators could question him about Mary.

Raoul was sad at the old lady's demise; he had enjoyed sparring with her and liked her frisky way of telling him to behave with Mary. He remembered her defending Mary like a mother protecting her young. Smiling at the thought of when she had manhandled him out of a room with her big body.

Unfortunately Ramsey's inquiries had grounded to a halt in their search for Mary or her whereabouts was concerned, they could not find anything worthwhile except that her records as a child had been closed by the children's court.

Raoul remembered what Mary had told him about her early childhood, and to this day he was haunted by how she came to have those horrific scars on her otherwise beautiful body. He didn't want to tell these facts to Ramsey but if it could help in the search for her, then so be it so he relayed the information to Leslie.

It was as though she had fallen off the face of the earth, all further enquiries drew a blank, but Leslie said now she knew more of Mary's earlier life, she would call in favours from a friend who worked in the judicial system for inside info. Raoul emphasised everything had to be above board, no shortcuts.

One afternoon Raoul received a phone call from his brother Louis, which made him feel guilty as he had not told his elder sibling of his involvement with Mary.

"Bonjour Louis, it is seven am in Paris, why are you phoning me so early in the morning brother, or are you just getting home?"

"Well you kept cancelling your trips to Paris so I have to pin you down somehow. Raoul, I have a great need for your support here as I am about to become engaged to get married to the most wonderful girl. I would appreciate your backing in this important step in my life, will you come?"

It felt like he had run into a brick wall, Raoul could not believe his ears. "Ha-ha very funny Louis, what woman in her right mind would want to voluntarily take you on as a husband. You're too much of a reprobate, does she know about your addiction for kinky sex, and about Filipina, or is that a stupid question?"

The laughter at the other end of the phone answered his question, "That is a stupid question, of course not, at least not yet, but I may introduce her to it on our honeymoon. She is a bit of a prude and only likes vanilla sex, but enough I have reserved your usual suite, unfortunately I am in Geneva at the moment but hope to return to Paris by this Friday. So can I expect you my brother, oui?"

"Certainly Louis, I would not miss this momentous celebration for anything, this I have to see with my own eyes. She must be a very special woman to have captured the heart of Paris's greatest playboy, what is her name, is she French?"

Raoul heard a woman's voice in the background,

"Is she with you in Geneva Louis?"

Laughing his brother said "No that is Filipina, my fiancée's name is Rose and she is as English as her name suggests. She is the most frustrating and beautiful woman I have ever met, you will love her on sight. She is a very busy business woman and sometimes even I cannot keep up with her global travels. Au revoir my brother and merci"

After his conversation with his brother Raoul moved to the drinks cabinet in his office and poured a good measure of whiskey, turning he looked down at the fast moving afternoon traffic, absently thinking about his brothers engagement to one woman while still involved with his long time mistress.

An English woman, hmm they were not known to be tolerant of the French way of mistresses as a second sexual mate. She must love Louis a lot to put up with his extra sexual partners, or maybe she does not know about his brother's allure for mixed couple's sexual interludes.

His own thoughts drifted to his behaviour since ending the relationship with Mary, hadn't he done the same thing, had an affair with Mary while still in a relationship with his own mistress, yes, and it still left a nasty taste in his mouth. Although he could have and did have any woman he wanted, the one thing he would not give them was sex. What would be the point of that futile exercise when he felt nothing for them, no sexual arousal, nothing?

So maybe this weekend he would find a beautiful partner and end his self-imposed celibacy.

———— ❋ ————

When he returned to Paris it was later than he expected, and he would have to hurry, thank goodness he changed into his tux on his private jet to save time. Landing at the section for private aircraft at De Gaulle airport, he took a moment to look at his place of birth. It always amazed him how much he missed the old girl, but he never felt that inclination when he was away from her.

Having a valet take his luggage up to the suite he squared his impressive shoulders; then made his way to the ballroom after enquiring his brother's whereabouts.

# Chapter 24

Walking between the beautifully decorated tables, and ignoring the flirtiest glances of the heavily made-up faces of the woman, he spotted his brother at the bar.

Standing at the bar after shaking his brother's hand, a happy smile on his face, Raoul picked up the glass of whiskey he ordered and raised it to his mouth when suddenly he stopped in his tracks unable to believe his eyes.

Mary had walked into the ballroom, Louis said in a jovial voice, about to go and meet her "Ah my Cherie, she has just arrived, come and meet Rose ..." Raoul grabbed Louis's arm, staying his progress.

"Wait, are you telling me that woman with the long auburn hair and in the black dress is your fiancée?"

Louis gave his young brother a questioning look "What's wrong, do you know her, but how is this when you live and work in Singapore, explain S'il vous plait?"

Raoul removed his wallet from his inner jacket pocket and showed Louis photos of both him and Mary, then went on to explain his relationship with Mary.

Louis is stunned, his hand shaking as he lifted the glass and drank the contents in one gulp. At his multiple questions, Raoul could see his brother's anger building, then he suddenly threw the glass on the bar and strode towards the woman he called Rose. Raoul saw she looked puzzled at the fury in her fiancée's eyes. Louis put his arm round his mistress and started dancing very sexily with her.

Raoul was sickened by his brother's next actions and he could see the hurt reflected in Rose's face by her body language. It gave him a sense of satisfaction as he leaned over her shoulder and said between gritted teeth.

"What you're feeling now is how I felt when I watched you do the same dance with another man; I hope the image stays in your mind just like it has in mine, even in your sleep"

Then wanting to feel the euphoria he always felt one last time, he kissed her cheek ... and felt nothing. But wait, that cannot be right he should have been aroused by now but no, he felt nothing.

A man with shocking red hair stepped between them and lifted a glass of liquid to her mouth "Come on Rosey girl, breathe" She looked at the man, her eyes glazed.

The dance finished then the pair left the floor arm in arm and moved out to the balcony.

Raising pain filled eyes she tried to focus "Oh William, Lucille ... why?" Her voice was thick and clogged with tears that found release, leaving a trail down her beautiful cheeks.

Raoul wanted to touch this woman again, just to see if he really felt nothing, but the woman called Lucille moved in front of him and hugged Rose, the guests interested at what was going on around them.

Yes, Raoul was disgusted by his brother's behaviour, questioning himself why he did not wait to tell Louis in private, this was not the outcome he wanted.

Yes, he was extremely angry at this woman, but to humiliate her like this on her engagement, in front of hundreds of their guests was not the act of a gentleman.

Yes, Raoul had always prided himself to act properly in public, with the one exception when he tried to make Mary jealous with his actions in Singapore that was an act of revenge.

Louise and his partner returned, and Raoul again looked at the woman, trying, but not succeeding to relinquish the thought this was his Mary.

Seeing the hurt on his ex-fiancée's eyes, Louis invaded her private space "As you had an affair with my own brother, I withdraw my proposal; I no longer want you as my wife. I hope it hurts, serves you right" He jeered in her face, throwing lewd accusations at her, which caused her body to stiffen in revulsion at his words.

Suddenly her hand shot out and she slapped Louis across the face, he staggered back a pace, totally surprised by her action. His face contorted but before he could retaliate, the woman called Lucille pushed him away. The anger emanating from her could be felt all round the room as she went to the woman called Rose's defence with all guns blazing.

What transpired was a revelation even to Raoul. He could not take in all the intimate evidence that was being shown to everyone in the room, of the love and protection this Lucille was given to her sibling.

Louis interrupted her tirade "This is my brother Raoul; this despicable woman had an affair with him, then found out I was the richer brother so she dropped him ..." Raoul waved his hand in front of Louis's face.

"That is not what happened, I ended the relationship ..." Lucille shouted at the pair of them "Shut up you morons, Rose do you know this man ...?" Raoul spoke over her

"She was calling herself Mary; she was a florist and was adopted by a woman called Mrs Grant …"

Spinning on her heel, the woman called Lucille shouted in his face while poking him in the chest with a very hurtful finger. "You're a lying scumbag, my mum and dad were Rose's foster parents at the age of five she has been my sister all these years"

"If anyone is lying it's her" Raoul moved to touch Rose on the shoulder and the next moment he's on the floor, with his arm held by Rose at a very dangerous angle, and his wrist bent in the opposite direction.

She also had the heel of one of her shoes pressed against his throat. He could hear the other people and Louis shouting at her, but it was the coldness of her voice that reached him.

"Move an inch and I'll break your arm, no one abuses me ever again" The man with red hair spoke gently to her and she relaxed her hold on Raoul, allowing him to move off the floor.

Jumping to his feet, he rubbed his aching shoulder, and thought this is all wrong; his

Mary would never hurt another person. Although he could not verbally say without a doubt *yet* that this woman was *not* his Mary, but he already knew in his gut she was not her.

Oh, she was just as beautiful in features, but he felt nothing, zilch, there was still anger in his heart so she wore it when he saw Mervin and Carlos move to her side.

"I see you still have both your lovers hanging ..." Marvin interrupted his speech and moved swiftly right into Raoul's face "Insult my friend and my husband again and I will stab you in your worthless heart"

"I saw her dance the forbidden dance with him" Raoul nodded at Carlos.

"Yes at my request as I can't dance, we have loved Rose since forever, but tell us, did you see her kiss him at the finish of the dance like this piece of garbage did, did he take her outside and have filthy sex up against the wall as this cretin surely had by the state of their undress?" Shaking his head Raoul replied "No, she kissed him on both cheeks"

"Exactly you spineless worm, now move

before my husband puts you permanently in one of our hospitals that our Rosy girl sponsors" The man named William spoke softly to Rose who still looked shell-shocked, then she nodded.

William took the podium and what he related to the assembled guests made Raoul feel shame.

He looked at this woman who had suffered pain in her young years, but through her inner strengths, very smart work, and friends, of course with her sister and foster families love, she has succeeded.

Before leaving the ballroom Rose confronted the brothers and vowed vengeance by going after their assets. She would start immediately on Lafette banks, then Louis's private fortune. She told Raoul she would give him some leeway and if she didn't get a written apology in all the international newspapers from both of them, she would take them down, penny by penny if she had too.

———— ✹ ————

Raoul sat at his desk in his office in Singapore, his head not on his business, but on the invitation in his hand, he could not believe that Rose Faraday was actually in Singapore for a symposium.

Dressing that evening with care he set off with hope in his heart that she may have knowledge of where his Mary was even if he knew it was a long shot, because she would not answer his other channels of enquiries, hence this face to face confrontation.

When Ramsey had requested an interview with her, they were turned down saying she awaited his apology, the longer that took the more time she had to bring him down.

Raoul had already rescinded his orders to all his staff about any calls from Mary, he wanted all calls or any information they received from other sources to be given to him directly. He realised it might be too late but he would keep trying, no, he needed to keep trying.

Later that night as he listened to this magnificent woman address the young entrepreneurs in their own language he was amazed by her acumen; she was a first class business woman, he knew he would fight her tooth and nail to get the info he required about his Mary.

Alas, when he approached her she blew him off until he apologised to her in all the international newspapers about his handling of the situation at her engagement in Paris.

This was one very strong woman

He left without the information he craved.

It was seven months since Raoul's meeting with Rose in Paris, when she made it clear to him she was going all-out to attack his companies if she didn't get the apology she requested, she gave him two months leeway to comply then she would start the proceeding.

Rose had already commenced her assault on the Lafette banking businesses, with devastating results.

The directors of the bank pleaded with Raoul to convince Louis that ignoring the danger to the bank was letting their shareholders down, as Rose had already bought up quite a few of the dissatisfied member's shares.

They requested Louis stand down as chairman, stating he was rarely at the bank and refused to take the danger of a hostile take-over seriously, they insinuated he had lost his initiative and was incompetent after the debacle with his long-term mistress.

Raoul pleaded with Louis to take the situation at more seriously, to protect the shareholders investments and his own personal fortune, to help defend the workers' jobs in all of the Lafette businesses.

Unfortunately it was like talking to a brick wall as Louis had no intention of apologising to *that* woman now or in the future, even when Raoul explained the woman named Rose had not been the same woman Raoul was involved with.

He refused to listen to Raoul or take the threat seriously that he could lose everything that generations of Lafette family had worked hard for.

Also he had started drinking heavily.

Raoul was disheartened by Louis behaviour, his brother was being unreasonable, but he could not let it interfere when he started his own fight to protect his own businesses. All he could do was to be there for when Louis needed him.

He had Ramsey's do an investigation into Rose's multiple businesses, but her port folios were vast, coming under different names. He should not have been astounded at the shrewdness Rose showed in her commerce, nor after hearing in Singapore what she had accomplished in her young life.

How could he ever have thought this woman was his Mary? His Mary was gentle, loving, a calming influence on a stressed personality, oh she could be a spitfire when cornered as he had experienced it on the night he broke up with her.

Yes, she had gone toe to toe with him the day he accused her of being unfaithful.

How wrong he had been, my God he wanted her in his life so badly; he missed her every day, suddenly he threw himself out of his office chair, phoned down for the valet to bring his car up from the garage, and then told his PA he was finished for the day.

She knew better than to argue with her boss when his mind was made up, even though meetings were scheduled back to back. Arriving home, he changed into sweatshirt and joggers and trainers then he hit the gym in his basement. It was the only way he could forget for a little while in his exhaustion what he had lost.

His Mary

He made a promise in his heart, to find his love.

# Chapter 25

Mary and the Rainbow Gardens Horticultural Club, as the people employed at Rainbow Gardens were now known, had brought work to the small town and to a lot of its young unemployed.

The enthusiasm of the youngsters to learn gave the older generation a new lease on life and filled them with the need to teach them how to love mother earth.

Mary had to leave a lot of the fruit picking and replanting to others and do a quieter job in the office as she was not carrying her baby well.

Doctor Fleming was worried about Mary's high blood pressure and continuous morning sickness that lasted nearly all day, and was making life difficult for Mary, plus the small shows of blood, so under doctor's orders she was practically on permanent bedrest.

These were the times Mary couldn't stop her thoughts turning to Raoul, she missed him, wanting his strength and support to help her through this worrying time. Even the card he had given to her early in their relationship with his personal phone number had been disconnected.

Mrs Grant's old housekeeper and her husband wanted to stay on with Mary when she had taken over the ownership of the property, and she was eternally grateful for as they were a God's send.

Betty handled Mary with kid gloves except when she was doing too much then Betty upped the ante and refused to listen to Mary's explanation and shunted her off to bed to rest. Betty kept the house spick and span, none of the men, including her husband, were allowed to enter the house with their muddy boots, she soon gave them short shift and sent them around the back of the house to the wet room.

Dave acted as chauffer when needed, but mostly he looked after the mechanics of the house cars and the trucks and tractors belonging to the estate with the help of a young apprentice from the village.

Pushing open her bedroom door, Mary moved to the adjoining dressing room that Betty and Dave had made into a nursery for the new baby. Mary did not want to use the official nursery as it was too far away; she wanted to be near her baby, and within hearing.

Betty and Mary had painted the room in lovely shades of lemon with pale green trim, while soft net curtains blew higilty-pigilty with the freezing breeze coming through the partially open window.

A giant giraffe was standing proudly in one corner, a gift from Lily and a chocolatey brown bear sat in the large rocking chair near the baby's change table. A small wicker cot was placed near the window, draped in white and lemon blankets.

Mary had used stencils to outline

various animals in different action poses on one wall with a magnificent rainbow surrounded by an assorted of birds, trees and a variety of beautiful flowers.

Then on another wall she depicted clouds drifting amongst twinkling stars, with a sleepy moon yawning.

Patting her very large belly, she spoke tenderly to her baby "Not long now my lovey, then I will show you all the love I never had. You will learn to give love back and grow with it. I just wish your father could be here, he really isn't a bad man, and yes I admit this to only you how much I love him for all his faults and arrogance. Maybe in time he will realise what he's missing and come home to us"

So Mary awaited her baby's arrival with some trepidation, and excitement.

Three years later.

The last three years had been gruelling for Mary, helping the men with the arrangements for the charity fete for the maternity unit in the local hospital. Directing them where to put the large tents, a bouncing castle for the children or any adventurous adults, Mary knew it would be a big success.

The stall holding the laughing clowns with their mouths open, the stalls with the hoops to win prizes, and lots more also the fruit and vegetables and cake stalls, optimistically enticing to part people from their hard earned money.

Mary would open her home and gardens to the public for this event in two weeks' time, hoping her piece de resistance would be the topiary sculptures, started by Mr Grant's forbearers, and carried by Mr Grant with pride, there were elephants with their trunks up for good luck, cats, dogs, mice, a giraffe, an aeroplane, two little girls playing, and lots more.

Keeping busy was what Mary needed just now, as for the past week she had strange dreams about her beautiful rainbow appearing over a building with a shield in the front gate, painted black and white. Then in another dream her rainbow had a hand pointing to a fountain held up by children.

Also she had uncanny feelings of something important about to happen and they were getting stronger every day. Looking on the internet she found the building was St Bartholomew's Hospital.

So here she was on the train to London with a sense of hurry in her movements. Taking a taxi from Fenchurch Street station to the hospital, Mary drew a big breath as she walked up to the information desk and joined the queue, suddenly she was pulled into an embrace, shocked she tried to break free.

"Oh you smart girl Rose, but what are you doing out of bed and dressed, come on take me to my gorgeous nephew, why what's the matter Rose?"

Backing away from the very heavily pregnant redheaded woman, Mary was about to answer her when a nurse came running up to Mary taking her arm exclaiming "Oh my goodness Mrs Wendell, you shouldn't be down here, standing about. I've been looking everywhere for you, please come back to your room"

Hands on her hips Mary stood her

ground, "I think you have the wrong person, my name isn't Rose or Mrs Wendell" The pregnant lady took Mary's hands saying "Hi Mary, my name is Lucille, and we have been looking for you for years. Rose is my step-sister, and your twin sister who gave birth this morning to your nephew. Mary please would you like to meet your long lost sister?"

Tears in her eyes Mary nodded. Lucille led the way to the maternity unit saying "If you don't mind I'd like to ask where you have been living, my sister had private investigators looking for you for years?"

Shocked by this information Mary replied "For years, but I don't understand, how did she even know she had a sister. I thought I was an orphan" Shaking her head Lucille said "Wait till you meet her Mary, she is a very special woman, and it's amazing how many of her attributes you have, your mannerism are exactly like hers, even to your voice. Here we are Mary please let me go first and introduce you?"

Knocking on the door Lucille walked in, she stood in front of Mary to block her from view. "Hi Rosey girl how are you, trust you to beat me to having your baby first. Ah hi William, Rose I have a very special friend I'd like you to meet, can she come in please?"

Standing aside, Mary walked forward, and Rose let out a scream and flew out of the bed tears streaming down her face. She grabbed hold of Mary, kissing a face as familiar as her own. "I knew it, I knew you existed, very rarely does my feeling let me down. I was praying all through my delivery that you would hear my thoughts and prayers. You are real aren't you, oh of course you are? Oh my God William she found us" Rose reached out for her husband's hand while keeping a tight hold of Mary.

"Rosey girl let the woman breathe, your squeezing her to tight, hi Mary I'm William, this lovely crazy woman's adoring husband and dotting father to our little miracle son, William Jr, Jr' At Mary's quizzical look he said "I'll explain later. Come on Rosey, back into bed with you, your exhausted"

Rose clutched Mary's hand tightly, "You won't go away will you, please stay till I have a nap please Mary say you'll stay?" Laughing through her tears Mary sat down in the chair next to her sister's bed "Sleep in peace my sweet sister, I'm not going anywhere" And she watched as Rose succumbed into an exhausted sleep.

"May I see your son William?" Mary looked into the cot as he moved to the other side "Why he's the spitting image of my daughter when she was a baby, except for the red hair. Poor boy he's going to be teased about that. He's gorgeous William, you must be so proud"

Turning to Lucille, Mary asked "When you first saw me you called me by my name, how did you know I was Mary?" Smiling Lucille was about to answer when she bent over, her face screwed up in surprise.

"Oh boy William, I think my water just broke, I have had some minor contractions earlier today, can you call Jason please he is in court today, I think you had better hurry as I'm having another contraction" This was said through gritted teeth.

Mary pressed the buzzer for a nurse while William tried to get a hold of Lucile's husband. As the nurse entered she took one look at Lucille and said "Well now, we better get you into a hospital gown and then see how far along you are"

As the door closed on them, Willian suggested a nice cup of Earl Grey tea "There is a small kitchen on this floor for patients use, I presume you take the same tea as Rose?" Looking at his wife asleep for the first time since giving birth this morning, she said she didn't want to miss a minute of their son's life.

"We need some self-time together Mary" Following him Mary said "Oh yes please, I'm parched, William will Lucille be alright, I know what it's like to give birth with no one there to support you"

He carried the tray of tea, coffee and wrapped biscuits into a visitor's room. "Why Mary, Lucille is not, nor will never be on her own. She had family here to help her. There's Rose, Jason, me, and now you"

Tears never seemed far away for her today, maybe all the excitement was finally getting to her. "William, I have yearned all my life for a family, now I have a big family to call my own, thank you" He was amazed how like his wife she was, even when she moved her hands to describe something, to drinking the same tea, even having the same sexy laugh.

Smiling he said "We have a lot to discuss Mary, it will take time, so why don't you just get to know your sister then we can explain how this came about, okay?"

The door slammed open and a man strode into the room. "So this is where your hiding William, hey Rose should you be out of bed so soon, you clever girl, a boy. Wait a minute you're not our Rosey, who is... Oh God your Mary, jeez you're so like our Rosey. Must be off my Lucille is in the throes of giving me a baby, see you all later" then he was gone.

Laughing Mary said "I'm assuming that was Jason, Lucille's husband?" Nodding as he got up William said "Time to look in on my wife and baby, come with me Mary, I dare not let you out of my sight, my wife you skin me if you got away"

Pausing outside his wife's door William took Mary's hands in his "I know we have a lot to talk about Mary and I for one would like to know all about you, but because of Lucille and Rose's present situation we need to wait for the right moment and now is not the time, do you agree?" Nodding Mary said "Later then William, when events have settled down"

# Chapter 26

Driving up the driveway between tall poplars in the early afternoon, he viewed the most beautiful and tranquil house he had ever seen, surrounded by well-kept lawns and gardens. Raoul sat for a moment in his low slung sports car enjoying the calm, because the storm he knew he would have to face would be explosive. He looked around observing the landscaping, and the unique terraced gardens with interest.

It had taken him longer than anticipated to locate Mary, he never knew about this place.

It had taken one of Ramsey's new staff members to look outside the square and investigate *Mr* Grant's background. His pulse was racing, he felt alive for the first time in three years because he knew his Mary was near.

Just then a movement caught his eye, he move forward and saw her, his Mary, his love.

He prayed like he'd never prayed in his life.

Mary had heard the sound of the car on the gravelled driveway, rising from the dirt she had been digging in, she clasped her hands together, of course she recognised the car immediately, and her heart began to pound in her breast.

'Hmm, it took him long enough' Mary thought as she tried to clean her face with dirty hands as well as her shirt and not succeeding? Looking down at her dowdy cloths she knew she was not dressed as she would have like to be for this awkward meeting.

Then straitening her shoulders, she thought 'This is me, like it or leave it. Then pleaded in her heart, please like *me*' as he walked towards her. Her look turned to amazement. 'Is this the immaculate man she loved?' His bespoke cloths hung on his body, his hair overly long, and his usually clean shaven face sporting dark stubble.

Raoul smiled at this action, yes that was his Mary, doing what she loved best, mucking around in the dirt, and for the first time in years he felt at peace as he looked at the woman he loved and lost through his stupidity and arrogance. He thought, 'Please let her listen, to let him explain, to make his atonement.'

His heart breaking at what he had put the gentle innocent woman through, yes it was time to eat his own foolish words.

Walking forward, he stopped a few inches, trying to formulate some sort of greeting then decided to tell the truth.

"Mary, will you please give me a hearing. I would like to tell you something of my younger days; this is not an excuse for my atrocious behaviour towards you, although it did set me on a path of behaviour for the future as the man I would become, as in how I would live my life"

Nodding her consent in silence, Mary heard his sad story.

At the end he shoved his hands into his pockets, and paced a little away from her, then turned back to her, his voice beseeching.

"Mary, you are the first woman I have allowed to get near me, oh I do not mean physically, I mean in my heart, when I thought you had betrayed me, I went crazy. So I deliberately let you believe there was something going on with me and Leslie, but the truth is she is a lesbian, always has been and the day you saw us at the hotel, she required some recovery time as she'd had IVF treatment and was pregnant. When you saw us at the hospital, she'd had a scan and was informed she was carrying a son"

Searching her face for some reaction to his words but Mary kept her eyes downcast.

"When I saw you in the family's hotel I fell headlong in love with you, for me it was love at first sight, and I have never recovered. I hurt every day for the pain I've caused you; I have never had sex with any women since you. I ask you, no damn it Mary I'm begging you for your forgiveness?"

Raoul stretched his hands out in an

319

imploring manner, Mary lifted her head, sweeping her tangled hair from her flushed face and gazed at his finely manicured hands then she raised her eyes to look at the first and only man she had ever felt emotion for. This was the man who had ruined her reputation and deprived her of her livelihood, who had shut her out of his life, who had left her alone and pregnant.

He was the man who threw her love back in her face, and all she could see was his anguish, not only in his huge weight loss, but in his drawn features and the pain reflected back at her from his pleading eyes.

Suddenly she felt a tremendous kick in her heart and knew she could not continue to give back hurt for hurt, only she could stop this here and now. She no longer wanted to live without this man. Her body recognised him, her heart had been weeping for him, now it demanded him and she wanted, desired and needed him.

Period

Mary is surprised when Raoul grabbed her hand and opened her palm, and then closing her fingers over it murmuring in a cajoling voice "Remember this, when I asked you to keep it safe for me until I reclaimed it properly, with love, well I want it back now please, please my Mary?"

His wavering smile just melted her heart but it was the sheen of tears in his eyes that did the trick and she desperately wanted to touch him. "I should make you grovel for the hurt you inflicted on me, but Mrs Grant was a great teacher in granting forgiveness, she taught me well, saying not to let my earlier sad life hold me back from having a future my love, now I have a lovely surprise for you" Then she gave him her open palm and said "You may claim your kiss, with my heartfelt love"

Just as he was about to gather her in his arms, he saw her look over his shoulder, turning round he saw a tall man with a slight limp moving in their direction.

Oh God was he too late, is this man her husband? Then her words sank into his brain, and relief flooded his whole being. She had called him her love; he would never let her go.

Hang on; he took a longer look at the

man. "Hello, don't I know you, ah yes your David Holt, the manager of my Mayfair hotel" Raoul's gaze held a question as he turned back to Mary. "Raoul there is a lot I need to tell you, but it will have to wait a while as we have visitors" Nodding at another car as it approached the house.

It was the expression on Mary's face that captured Raoul's attention; she had lit up like a Christmas tree, then a little whirlwind of a body was flying out of the front door of the house, her tawney hair flying behind her, arms stretched out in front of her sturdy little body, squealing in delight as she jumped up and down on the spot obviously recognising the cars.

David walked away from Mary, catching the small child in his arms as he turned towards the new arrivals, but the child had other ideas, "Down Dabey down pease?" She screamed.

Scrambling away she rushed headlong at the newcomers, "You comed, I lub you all, come on hurry up?" The little girl shouted.

Raoul surveyed the group of people then squared his shoulders, he knew he was in for a rough time from them, but nothing was going to stop him from completing his heart's desire.

Turning, he looked at the love of his life and felt shame for having left things too late? But by God he was not leaving without a fight … wait what had she said, Mrs Grant had taught her forgiveness. She had called him her love.

"Mary oh God Mary, I love you so much"

"Hush my love; we will work this out together later. Come let me introduce you to my twin sister and your daughter" The shocked look he gave her caused her to pause momentarily.

By now the visitors had reached them. Taking her sister's hand she said "Let's all go and sit out on the back patio, I think this calls for a nice cup of tea and then we can explain to Raoul how we found each other and what we found out "Grumbling under his breath Jason said "You have to be joking, I prefer a man's drink, David will you do the honours"

As they all gathered around the large table that had a variety of food on it, David moved to the bar and passed Jason a beer. "Now that's a man's drink, what are you all laughing at?" His wife Lucille, was laughing the hardest, "Don't ever change my sweet" she begged.

Raoul's eyes never left the children as the girl crouched down to play with the little boy and girl crawling on the floor. The small girl appeared to be the leader, her hands flying everywhere and talking in an excited voice over the other children's baby talk.

A woman appeared with a tray of mixed drinks for the children, then a man carrying another tray with cups and saucers and tea pots. David sat down with a beer and watched Raoul, deciding to put him out of his misery.

"I am just a friend of the family, and so is Estelle my wife when she is at home, and not abroad with the Doctors without Borders, these good people have allowed me to share in the joy of their children as my wife and I can't have any, hopefully that will answer your questions about my presence here"

"I never asked you any questions but I appreciate you telling me, thank you" Raoul could now concentrate on who's who. Just then the little girl with the bright auburn hair who had been observing him moved closer little by little and then stopped, her tongue touching her top lip. Leaning on his knees with her bony elbows she asked "Hello I'm Rosemary, are you my Daddy?"

# Chapter 27

The talking at the table stopped suddenly, the silence was deafening, and everyone watching and waiting for him to answer the little girl. Slowly he turned to look towards Mary, her beautiful eyes swimming with tears as she nodded her head.

He touched the girl on the head, clearing his throat "Bonjour mon enfant, oui I am definitely your Papa and I am very happy to meet you, will it be possible for you to give me a hug?"

The child whooped with joy and scrambled onto his lap and gave him a big hug, her smile showed a dimple on her left cheek as she shouted "That is one of my super-duper biggest squeezes and it's all for you cause I lub you, hi everybody this is my daddy and he has come home to me cause he lubs me to" Then she hesitated, her tongue playing with her top lip "Pease what was that funny thing you said to me?"

Smiling through his tears he replied "I said hello, my little one, yes I am your father"

"Pease don't cry, I lub you to" And she wiped his eyes with her fingers. Mary's chair scrapped the stone floor as she pushed out of it, intending to shoo the children out but David beat her to it "Come on rascals, we need to let your parents have big people talks, let's go and scare the heebie-jeebies out of Aunty Lily and raid the kitchen" The little girl giggled and followed him like the pied piper, the smaller children crawling as fast as their tiny legs would go.

Rose paced the floor for a minute, then said "Ok I will start" Touching the red haired man next to her she said "This wonderful man is my husband William Wardell, you may recall meeting him once, he is in finance and the little tuff boy is our son William Jr Jr. Ok I will explain the joke, This distinguished gentleman is William senior, my Williams father, my William is Jr and our son is William Jr Jr, hence the joke, ok that fell flat"

When everyone stopped laughing Rose carried on with the introductions "This life saver is Lucille, my sister-by- choice and her husband Jason whom you have also met; he is a lawyer and their gorgeous daughter Hope. You know about David. So, if you remember the last time we meet was at the symposium in Singapore, I have to say it took you long enough to apologise, thank you for that. You fought a good fight."

Then she gave him a quizzical look, "Shame your brother took the hard road, but that was his choice, I hear he is in a sanatorium drying out" Raoul realised that was a statement, not a question.

Leaning over she put her hand out to him, never hesitating for a moment Raoul shook hands and knew an agreement had been established with this amazing young woman.

"Now to our story" Rose looked over at Mary, who gave her the go-a-head.

"Through a lot of investigations William managed to track down the midwife who delivered us. She was a bit forgetful, but she remembered us, and explained about our birth. Our mother died during our delivery on a very bad stormy night, so there was no information pertaining to us. The midwife saw a flower tattooed on her arm, so she called me Rose and my sister Mary, I was born first by two minutes, so I'm the eldest, stop laughing Jason" And she punched his arm playfully.

"To continue, the cottage hospital was old and ready to be pulled down, so it never had computers installed. On the night we were born it was struck by lightning and caught fire; all the patients had to be moved and ended up in different hospitals. We got separated in the move, and the nurse had been injured helping to fight the fire so she didn't realise what happened to us"

Pausing for a moment to drink some of her Earl Grey tea, she looked steadily at Raoul "Keeping up so far?"

He nodded "Please continue" Mary reached out to take his hand, squeezing it; he lifted it to his lips.

"Ok, I was sent to different foster homes, not good ones I have to say, I had put a teenager in hospital when I was four years old, then I ended up in Lucille's family when I was five. They gave me the first love I had ever known, and through that caring I am where I am today. Then I meet your brother then you and I have to say that was a revelation. Because of the fracas during that meeting it made William realise maybe there could be a twin somewhere, but it took a hell of a long search for the answers to be revealed, the rest you know"

Everyone watched his reaction to Rose's story, but Raoul watched Mary, who was drinking her tea; trying not to fidget in her chair. "Right my turn, I really don't want to relive what I went through but to get you to understand me I will have to tell you." Rose moved towards Mary and gave her a squeeze an encouraging smile. "My super-dupest squeeze sweet Mary"

Seeing the two women close together for

the first time, it was like seeing two peas-in-a-pod. Both were curvaceous, both had the same hair colour, both were the same height, the only difference was their speech; Mary still had a slight cockney twang.

Placing her cup on the saucer, Mary forced a smile to her stiff face and drew a deep breath "I was also sent to different foster homes, I only recently found out in one of the homes I had been sexually assaulted when I was five years old; that is why I wasn't a virgin, Also I had been beaten with a belt, and burned with cigarettes. So I ran away and lived on the streets until I was eight and Mrs Grant found me"

At this explanation Raoul exploded from his chair and swore fluently in French. Reaching for Mary he pulled her into his arms.

"No Mon Dieu, no my Cheri, I cannot comprehend this. Mary my sweet Mary, oh God you were but a child" And he dropped to his knees, hugging her legs, sobbing. The rest of the group silently made their exit after a gesture from Mary.

Bending down, Mary tugged him to his feet, her heart aching at hearing his distress.

"Raoul I love you, and I always have. It was hard at first because I didn't understand why I didn't like men, but you persevered and won my heart. After I found out I was pregnant, it was difficult to contact you in the first few months because no matter what I did I could not get past your very efficient staff to tell you about the baby, so I gave up. But when I started haemorrhaging and I nearly died I promised myself no matter what happened between us, you had to know about our baby, and I vowed to wait for you. I convinced myself you would feel my love and come for us. Mrs Grant always said if you pray hard enough and never lose your love, somehow it will come back to you. So I never gave up on you Raoul" She gently wiped his tears away

"Mary I have loved you from the moment I saw you in the family hotel, and my love just kept growing. When I mistakenly saw you doing that dance I thought you had betrayed me, then the engagement was the final straw, I went crazy. Under no circumstances did I ever think there could be two of you. There could only ever be one of you as you're the one who makes me feel alive, who makes me happy in every way, you are my heartbeat, without you my heart would wither and die. Mary if it takes the rest of my life I will show you every day how much I love you. Please I beg your forgiveness my Mary"

Snuggling up to his warm body Mary murmured, "I can't even do a soft-shoe shuffle never mind a fancy dance"

Crushing her ample body he just held her. He saw her other family members returning and he got down on one knee "Mary my love will you please, please forgive me, as only your love will heal me. I love you, I will always love you, you are my beating heart please my darling will you marry me and be my forever love?"

Mary looked at her family, her sister mouthing yes, yes her daughter kneeling beside her daddy holding her other hand, and Mary could swear she saw her rainbow in her happy tears, "I will forgive you my love and welcome to our family, yes please

I would love to be your wife and love you forever"

Holding her beloved in her arms she vowed they would live happily ever after, even if her daughter was trying to squeeze between them saying "Me too, me too pease" Raoul lifted his daughter up and wrapped them both in his strong arms, "For ever to infinity my dearly loved girls"

❋

# About the Author

Dorothy was born in Scotland, she wrote diaries to help her with an unhappy childhood. After settling in Queensland Australia, she worked at various jobs and raising her children left little time for R&R. Then she met a gentle friend Brian, who later became her loving partner for many years. They traveled far and wide, but after Australia his greatest country of choice was Scotland. After the loss of her partner Dorothy tried to recapture the romance she lost in writing. Now this was a great challenge to her and she asks her readers to excuse her naivety with her characters. All she wants to do is give her readers a while in make-believe fantasy.

Printed in the United States
By Bookmasters